Love
without
Color

Love
without
Color

RAJEANEE CHEEKS

LOVE WITHOUT COLOR

iUniverse books may be ordered through booksellers or by contacting:

iUniverse
1663 Liberty Drive
Bloomington, IN 47403
www.iuniverse.com
1-800-Authors (1-800-288-4677)

Because of the dynamic nature of the Internet, any web addresses or links contained in this book may have changed since publication and may no longer be valid. The views expressed in this work are solely those of the author and do not necessarily reflect the views of the publisher, and the publisher hereby disclaims any responsibility for them.

Any people depicted in stock imagery provided by Getty Images are models, and such images are being used for illustrative purposes only. Certain stock imagery © Getty Images.

ISBN: 978-1-5320-7097-6 (sc)
ISBN: 978-1-5320-7098-3 (e)

Library of Congress Control Number: 2019903324

Print information available on the last page.

iUniverse rev. date: 03/22/2019

CHAPTER 1

Welcome! My name is Makira Johnson. I'm a professor at Oliver Johnson University. I was born and raised in the streets of Biloxi, Mississippi—you know, that Magnolia State, southern slang, fried chicken, corn bread, and okra!

Now, what you are about to encounter is a sexy, thirty-year-old, five-foot-seven butter pecan African American in size 18 jeans—real meat, not that artificial butt-shot stuff. I'm a curvaceous, Afropuff-wearing, strong-minded, intelligent, stern, loose-lipped, nononsense, independent diva! If you didn't know yet, I'm talking about me, finding myself caught between love and a hard place! Do I follow my heart or follow protocol?

After this experience, my life was never the same! So just sit back, relax, and enjoy my story, *Love without Color*!

"Good morning, class. Today, we will be finding and elaborating on the definition of the word *slavery* and what it truly means to you.

When someone says the word *slavery*, what's the first thing that comes to mind?"

"Bondage and chains," Kia responded.

"What do you think, Corey?"

"Damaged goods and Negros," Corey responded.

"Very detailed," I said to Corey. "All of these things are correct, but let's go further than that! Forget the big plantation, the 'white master,' the long, blistering days in the heat, picking cotton in the cotton field. If I may ask you, does slavery still exist today? What things make you feel that you are being enslaved? The topic for this month is emancipation from slavery. What, when, where, how, and why?

"Question 1, 'What was your enslavement?' Question 2, 'When did you feel that you were being or becoming enslaved?' Question 3, 'Where were you when you were enslaved?' To clarify question 3, it could be either physically or mentally or both. Question 4, 'How did it overpower you?' Last but not least, question 5, 'Why did you feel that you were captured into slavery?'

"The era I would like to visit is the 1920s, which is the Harlem Renaissance era. It was a smooth, cool-as-ice, twice-as-nice, iconic, soul-filling, expressional era for black African Americans. We all have invites as VIP guests. Coming not as our regular selves in the modern day but as artists. Out of all the gifted poets of this era, which one relates to you the most, and how are they positive role models to you? Keep in mind that you are to select the best artist that strongly relates to you because you will be role playing as well.

"How do you think black African Americans of that era overcame being enslaved and helped today's society? My answer would simply be African Americans standing up as individuals and as a whole gave empowering speeches and developed organizations, such as the NAACP and the Black Panther Society, to protect African Americans' equal rights. Making an irremovable stain or stamp on today's black society.

"The NAACP, the National Association for the Advancement of Colored People, is a civil rights organization founded in 1909 to fight prejudice, lynching, and Jim Crow segregation and to work for the betterment—underlining *betterment*—of people of color. Secondly, the Black Panthers. The Black Panthers Party for Self-Defense, otherwise known as the Black Panther Party (BPP), was established in 1966 by Huey Newton and Bobby Seale.

"These two leading revolutionary men created the national organization as a way to collectively combat white oppression. After constantly seeing black people suffer from the torturous practices of police officers around the nation, Newton and Seale helped to form Liberian leaders to help suffering black people.

"My first choice is everyone's favorite, Martin Luther King Jr., a man defined by his fight for equal rights in America. Also, a vocal visionary and motivational speaker.

"Another good supporter of the African American race was Malcolm X, who also emerged as a leading voice in the civil rights movement.

"In comparison, both leaders had similar motives, but to contrast the two, manhood-wise, the journey to freeing themselves from being enslaved really stood out to me drastically.

"Me, personally, I absolutely love that Malcolm saw what he had become—a street hustler, convicted of robbery, locked down, isolated from society—took on a new change of life. He utilized his time effectively, to rebuild a new structure of a black man.

"Day in and day out, he used an instrument called a dictionary. Malcolm X said, 'In my slow, painstaking, ragged handwriting, I copied into my tablet everything printed on that first page, down to the punctuation marks. I believe it took me a day. Then aloud, I read back, to myself, everything I'd written on the tablet. Over and over, aloud, to myself, I read my own handwriting,' Malcolm said.

"Those seven years in prison were the most cherished and remarkable moments of his life. He had reached a new horizon in his life. He knew that in order to be a leader, you must challenge yourself before challenging your competitor. A phenomenal man, in my words.

"In conclusion, today was in introduction to the emancipation from slavery. For the next two months, we will not just be researching and writing a profile on these brilliant-minded people; no, we are going to write a profile on ourselves and how we overcame or are overcoming slavery. Our next chat will be about who you have chosen and why."

"Is everything okay? You were a bit quiet today," I said to Kia.

"Yes, everything is fine!" Kia said with a fake smile and walked away.

Now before I go any further, I want to introduce you to my best, best, best friend, Sapphire. She is five foot eight with a slim and fit model's figure, hazelnut eyes, and silky long hair. She is very intelligent, funny, beautiful, and somewhat bashful but overall a loyal friend. Sapphire has been my best friend since sixth grade. We had our first menstrual cycle together, double date, you name it! Now she works as my assistant. We know everything about each other—well, at least I thought we did.

See, T. J. is another childhood friend as well and also Sapphire's ex-boyfriend. T. J. now is a successful lawyer for the law firm Emerson and Brown.

Not talking about my successful black brother, but before the success train, he was a garbage lawyer. He couldn't even get the innocent off. One day, he went to my father for help because my father was a successful, yet retired, lawyer to coach him and help him be as successful as he was.

Bam! I swear it was like two weeks, and out of nowhere, he started winning cases, left and right, right and left, while losing Sapphire's love. He became too busy, too overworked, too cocky, and downright arrogant. T. J. and Sapphire quickly broke up, and Sapphire started dating this mysterious man no one knows of.

He was in the military and had been stationed in Iraq for months. Leaving Sapphire behind, three months pregnant with his child, and she needed to go out on maternity leave because of complications.

Sapphire was in the process of helping me find a replacement assistant for her absence. It had been hard for her because sometimes I am hard to get along with.

"Makira, finally, after seven unsuccessful interviews, *finally*, I found the perfect match for you!" said Sapphire.

"Well, let me see the résumé," I said. "This résumé is wonderful! Set me up a phone interview first, immediately. This is the one."

"There's just one problem with him," Sapphire said, worried.

"I don't care. That one problem won't hurt anything. This man is perfect!" I replied. "Let's say Thursday at three. I'll be available. Thank you so much for finally finding the perfect match! Oh, look at the time! I must go! I'm supposed to meet Daddy at Mary Mahoney's Old French Restaurant."

Now, my father, Oliver Johnson, was well known in the state of Mississippi. As stated previously, he was a retired lawyer, formerly at Emerson and Brown. He was the interim president and CEO of the NAACP, the founder and CEO of Oliver Johnson University, and a member of the Blank Panther Society at this time.

"Hey, Daddy!"

"Hey, honey, how was your day?"

"It was great! Sapphire finally found the perfect match for me!" I proclaimed.

"Oh, that is good. Male or female?" Daddy asked.

"Daddy, stop now. Just look at the résumé before you start passing judgment!" I told him.

"This is a very impressive résumé. So, this is a man. Did you set up an interview with Mr. Christian?" Daddy asked, upset.

"Yes, Daddy, and it is perfectly fine!" I confirmed.

"Yeah, for you or me?" Daddy asked.

"Daddy, stop it now. You are being absurd. Just give him a chance," I implored.

"Well, I would like to do a personal interview myself, just to make sure that everything does check out. Anybody can put anything on a résumé," Daddy explained.

"Fine, Daddy, but just don't jump to conclusions, please. Okay, Daddy?" I said, wanting him to agree with me.

Daddy just smiled and started drinking his drink.

"We all know what that means!"

After two more drinks and a brief conversation, Daddy and I decided to depart from each other's company.

After driving to my beautiful $759,000, three-bedroom, three-bathroom, 3,675-square-foot, all-brick, luxe-decorated house with its spacious rooms and enormous front yard and backyard, I quickly washed, slipped into something more comfortable, and then jumped into my $10,000 Phyllis Morris canopy bed and wrote in my diary.

As I lie here, desperate for attention,

Mourning for loving arms to hold me and embrace me after a long day—

A long yet delicate kiss from you, my love.

When will my life begin? When will true love come rushing into my lonely, cold bedroom doors?

Alone for another night!

CHAPTER 2

The Interview

It was seven in the morning, and I was awakened from my lonely slumber by the sun's rays. I revealed myself to the mirror as I perfumed my bare body and then carefully perfected my natural locks. Topping off my body, I decorated my curves with a skintight red body-con dress.

"I'm beautiful! Could this be it?" I said to myself.

I opened my diary and put in my daily entry. "Could this mysterious man not only be my potential assistant but assist me in a long life of love and happiness—if I may say, my future soul mate, my husband?"

I smiled at what fate might bring. Excited, I left and drove off to work.

"Good morning, class. Hopefully everyone has chosen their role model. So today, we are ready to elaborate and have a deep connection with whomever you have chosen. Keep in mind this is not just about role playing or, if I may say, entertainment, but indeed, it is an image of yourself and how you have overcome or are overcoming barriers in your life.

"To conclude, I just got word that we have a two-hour slot live, which makes me have to choose, including myself, my current assistant, and my former assistant, Sapphire, if everything goes well, seven Harlem Renaissance activists. You will all be responsible for writing a well-organized, detailed portfolio of your Harlem Renaissance activist and yourself and how you two relate and come with a significant purpose. I want this portfolio to be written with good penmanship. If it is illegible or sloppy, I will reject your portfolio and you will receive an automatic F. So please keep that in mind. We are moving forward in our era of emancipation from slavery and entering the Harlem Renaissance.

"Now, moving on, what is the Harlem Renaissance? The Harlem Renaissance was a cultural, social, and artistic explosion that took place in Harlem, New York, spanning the 1920s. During that time, it was known as the 'New Negro Movement,' named after the 1925 anthology by Alain Locke ... The Harlem Renaissance was a rebirth of African American arts.

"So, why is the Harlem Renaissance so significant? 'The Harlem Renaissance was very significant because it marked a moment when white America started recognizing the intellectual contributions of blacks and on the other hand African Americans asserted their intellectual identity and linked their struggle to that of blacks around the world and planted the seeds for what would later become the civil rights movement and for the first time provide us with positive and beautiful images of black folks.'

"My favorite activist of the Harlem Renaissance era is Georgia Douglas Johnson, born in Atlanta, Georgia. She married in 1910 and moved with her husband to Washington, DC. Her husband died in 1925, leaving her as a single mother of two, working temporary jobs to help support her children. In 1916, Johnson published her first poems in the NAACP's magazine *Crisis*. One of my personal favorites is 'The Heart of a Woman.'

"Now, observe yourself! Every one of us has the ability to maximize our minds and to fulfill the gift that God has planted in us. The only true enemy we have is ourselves. I know we were supposed to be introducing our character, but we have run out of time. Next class, we will introduce ourselves and our characters' lives. Also, make sure that your portfolio is neat, well organized, and clear to your audience. Come with your A game!"

"Have you seen Kia? I called her, and she didn't answer my phone calls or texts," I said to Sapphire.

"No, I haven't. That's not like Kia. She never misses class. I'll look into it," Sapphire said.

"Please do! I'm getting worried!" I said, frightened.

"Don't worry; she may have just gotten sick. I'll check into it," Sapphire assured me. "Are you ready for the interview?" she questioned me.

"Yes, I am. Just have to get my sexy operator voice game on," I said, clearing my throat. "You can leave now; I got it from here," I said, kicking her out my office.

I continued to familiarize myself with Christian's résumé until it was time for his phone interview.

I called him.

"Hello!" Christian greeted me.

"Hello, this is Makira Johnson for Oliver Johnson University. I am calling about the job opening for the assistant professor position. Are you still interested in this position?" I asked.

"Yes, ma'am, I am," Christian replied.

Turned on by his deep, gentle, polite voice, I became very aroused.

"You really impressed me with your résumé. "You have participated in charity fundraising for less fortunate African American teens and gave thousands of dollars toward scholarships. The list goes on. Now, excuse me for being so blunt, but if you have all this money, why would you apply for this entry-level position? Why do you think you are the best candidate for the position?" I asked.

"Well, my grandfather blessed me in his will before he died— acres of land and millions and millions of dollars! Why be selfish when someone blessed me and I can bless others in need, especially my black African American race! The brutality against black African American people saddens me but makes me want to make a difference. If there's going to be a change in the community, let it start with me!" Christian stated. "I feel like a little schoolboy saying this, but I've been following your work from your self-published books, such as *The Art of Black African Americans* and *Black Lives and Beyond*. Best sellers! Also, your YouTube channel videos of your teachings at Oliver Johnson University and your extravagant speeches at the Black Panther and NAACP conferences! You are a self-made woman, and I love it! You're like the black Superwoman! I think I have a major crush on you! So, it would be a major honor for me to work side by side with you!"

Filled all the way up in my feelings, I said, "You have the job! I will call you later to schedule a day you can start!"

"That sounds great!" Christian pronounced.

Hanging up the phone, all I could imagine was a sexy, built black African American man, educated, polite, deep womanizing voice, and money! What else could I ask for?

I can't take it anymore! This thang is strong! I have to see him today. Forget tomorrow! I was thinking. So I called the smooth operator back and got us some one-on-one time at Mignon's Steak and Seafood restaurant. Why waste a perfectly good dress? Gucci is not cheap, y'all!

Sexy from the top to the bottom of my red bottoms, I waited patiently for Christian to arrive. I'd been imagining things about the man ever since I laid ears on his Barry White voice. *Lord, have mercy, the things he can whisper in my ears. I'm telling you, if this man comes in here with a bald head, Rick Ross beard, built from top to bottom … we talking so built that his shoulders got shoulder pads! Oh my God, his beautiful pearly whites! That's it for me! All hands on deck! Hold my underwear and bra because it is on! I won't be a thirty-year-old virgin for long!*

"Miss Makira Johnson! Nice to finally meet you!"

"Okay, nice to meet you. Now, if you don't mind, I am waiting for someone, and I don't want him to get any wrong ideas with you standing here," I said, trying to brush him away.

"Well, I think I'm the one you're waiting for, Miss Makira! I am Christian Christiano!"

"Hold up! Wait a minute! Who let in Casper the friendly ghost! I know I didn't put on these toe crunchers and this two-thousand-dollar dress for no white man! Girl!" I said, thinking out aloud.

"Excuse me!" Christian said.

"Yes! Excuse you, because you're white!" I said.

"And you are black! I'm glad we know our colors!" Christian said.

"I can't believe this. Look, the position has been filled!" I said angrily as I got up to proceed out of the restaurant.

"*What!* Because I'm white? You know what? You are one evil, stuck-up, heartless, bitter woman!"

"Well, let me sweeten things up for you!" I said as I threw my sweet tea in his face and left the restaurant!

Upset, mislead, and hurt, I laid in my bed and poured my heart out on the pages.

"Was I right, or was I wrong? Could the one I dismiss be my true love after all?"

CHAPTER 3

Reflection

Dawn came. I arose and felt so ugly. What I had done and become was terrifying.

I looked at the woman on the other side of the mirror, desperately trying to find myself. Crying within, I pulled out my diary to pour out my emotions.

Looking at the lines in my diary, I could only come up with one word that defined my actions. I wrote the word, "SAVAGE!" Following that, I wrote the meaning of each letter in the word:

S—Spiteful

A—Antipathetic

V—Venomous

A—Arrogant

G—Gory

E—Egregious

Covering my spiteful ways, I had put on my Mac foundation, followed by other makeup accessories and left for work.

While I was driving to work, Sapphire called me. Still mad at her for not telling me that my Reggie Bush was actually rapper Eminem, I thought she definitely deserved this greeting, "What in the *hell* were you thinking letting a white man even have a potential shot of working as my assistant? You know what the rules are, no white people! Remember what my father said, quote unquote, white people are our enemies! You let one white man in; next thing you know, they want to take over everything. You had me looking like a fool!" I screamed out to Sapphire.

"I was trying to let you know that, but you said, 'I don't care. I can overlook that little problem.' And to me, I don't see the problem! This man gave to the community and is willing to make the difference that some of our black people are not. I don't understand you and your father's theory about the whole 'White Man' deal. This man is overqualified, and you're not trying to give him a chance just because of the color of his skin. You know what. You and your father are as bad as the people who tormented our ancestors," Sapphire finished.

"I don't care how you put it, I rejected him. You need to find me a *black* replacement! Okay!" I told Sapphire.

"Okay. I'll meet you at the school," she angrily agreed with me.

Finally, we met up at the school, and Sapphire lashed out at me. "I'm sorry that Christian is not your 'Chosen One' because he has a skin pigmentation!"

"Taking off my professional hat right now! Do you think that if the shoe was on the other foot, Mr. Christian would let me or you even get a slight chance to work at a predominantly white university? We both know the only way we would get that position! Either we are putting out something and we aren't talking about no money, or you just have really good connections. Otherwise, no matter how good your résumé is or confident you are, at the end of the day, you are as black as the words on the résumé! They all see a black woman or black man who comes from the ghetto, who is trying to get ahead, and they *won't* let you!"

"You're brainwashed!" Sapphire shouted out at me.

"No, I am a realist. My father taught me very well what to expect from the white man, and don't never give them a chance," I said.

"That's not right, Makira," Sapphire said.

"Yes, it is, so drop it, Sapphire!" I screamed out. "Now, how is the pregnancy going so far?" I asked.

"It's going well. I just went to the doctor yesterday, and he said everything checks out fine. I just need to be easy on my feet!" Sapphire exclaimed.

"How is your boyfriend?" I asked. "Will he be home to assist you with the baby? You know a child needs both parents, not one! And hopefully you two will tie the knot before the baby comes. You don't want any bastard child! We have enough of those in society now!"

"No, Makira, he will not be home for the birth. He is on duty," Sapphire said, frustrated.

"Well, do you have any pictures of this mysterious man, because I am beginning to believe that this man was a one-night stand or just a sperm donor! I just don't understand! Everything with you and T. J. was so perfect. What happened that was so bad that you and T. J. couldn't reconcile the matter and get over it? Now, you're pregnant by this man no one knows of, that you are so deeply in love with. You aren't married to him. I don't understand it. It makes no sense!" I argued.

"Now, quote unquote, let me take my professional hat off! You wouldn't understand any of the matters with me and T. J., which really aren't any of your business anyway! And to clear the record, I am married! I don't wear it because I didn't want to hear your garbage or anyone else's. You know what, Makira, I love you like a sister, but you know why you are single and a virgin at the age of thirty? Because you are way too judgmental, your attitude stinks, and if it is not Makira's way, it's no way!

"You prance around here with your nose so far up in the air like you can't be touched because this is your father's university. Well, honey, I got news for you! You've been touched!" Sapphire said as she got in my face.

"No man, or woman, would want to touch you with a two-by-four, because you are a nasty individual, and you are going to die being an old, stuck-up, stubborn virgin! You are a *savage*, and God have mercy on your soul, Makira!"

For twenty minutes, I just sat there in shock!

Later, that day, Sapphire took it upon herself to go to Kia's house to check on her.

As she walked to the front door, all she could hear was a man moaning. She approached the door and began to knock. The moans became louder and louder.

The man became very aggravated with Sapphire knocking and said, "Yo, what the f—— you want? I'm busy!"

"My name is Sapphire, and I'm here to see Kia?" Sapphire replied.

"Well, I'm busy with her! You're going to have to wait!" he said.

The moans got louder and louder until there was complete silence.

Five minutes later, Sapphire was still at the door.

Kia came to the door with a fresh black eye.

Sapphire was devastated and said, "Kia, what happened? You know you don't have to deal with this?"

"I'm all right. I'll be at school next week."

Tears started to fall from Sapphire's eyes as she stated to Kia, "Don't do this again. We are on the right track. You are so close! Please, if you need help, I will help you!"

Kia started to cry silently, and before she could say anything, the man, Kia's baby's father, Kieron, walked to the door and said, "Aye, ho, everything is good over here, so mind yo business!"

He slammed the door in Sapphire's face. Sapphire cried softly as she walked away from the door.

Meanwhile, on the other side of the door, Kieron picked Kia up and placed her in the bed with him. He held her tight and said, "I am all you need! F—— an education!" as he opened her legs to go another round.

Kia cried as she looked at herself in the mirror. She couldn't even recognize her own reflection!

CHAPTER 4

A Favor for a Secret

Christian, so upset, went and talked to his father the next day about what happened.

"Okay, so first I had a phone interview with Makira. Everything was fine. I was feeling her; she was feeling me. We were on the same page, until the in-person interview. First, before I get started, I want to say that Makira is the most gorgeous woman I have ever laid eyes on. I've been following her for a long, long time. Through my college years and until now, I have been following her diligently. She is a brilliant, intellectual human being and carries herself with dignity and respect. Very knowledgeable about her culture and the trials and tribulations of her people. She was everything I would want in a wife, until I met her in person. My whole perspective changed. When she looked at me, you would have thought she'd seen a ghost! She just dissed me! Disqualified me for the position because I am white! Dad, I was totally done! Like this person I had looked up to, this honest, respectful, genuine, intelligent woman actually turns out to be a real *jerk*."

Christian's father, Jonathan, answered his question by stating, "Maybe it is not her fault. "Maybe she has been poisoned all her life about white people. I know who her father is personally, and he is the epitome of jerks around the world and plays the victim role very well. I know how to handle him! You should have told me this sooner. Just stay by the phone; at six this afternoon, you will get a phone call from Mr. Oliver Johnson himself. He *will* hire you, and you will enjoy your time at this university," Jonathan confirmed.

Christian said, unsurely, "Look, Dad, no offense, but Makira has made up her mind. I'm just done with it!"

Jonathan reassured his son, "Trust me; it will happen."

"Okay, Dad, well, just wanted to let you know what was going on in my world, and I'll see you later."

As Christian was leaving his father's office, Jonathan smiled at him to reassure his son that he would get the job.

It was five thirty in the evening, and Christian's father went to Oliver Johnson University to pay my daddy, Oliver, a visit with a special guest.

Christian's father entered his office and greeted him as he sat down in front of him.

"Hello, Mr. Oliver, how are you doing?"

"What are you doing here?" Daddy asked Jonathan.

"I'm here because I have a concern, and unfortunately, it deals with you and your daughter, Makira!" He looked straight through Oliver.

"I don't understand your concern!" Daddy said, confused.

"Don't forget who gave you the money to start this university! It was my *white* money that started this university. What will your people think when they learn that this university was invested in by a white man! Come on; let's stop beating around the bush. My son,

Christian, has applied here and was accepted and then denied. I know that my son has all the qualifications needed for this position. Now this brings a great concern to me. I know and he knows that he is not getting the job because he is white."

"In that case, that's a big *no, no!*"

"Then I will have to expose you for who you really are! This almighty Black Panther leader, in his spare time, picks up *white* prostitutes and does horrific sexual activities with them." Jonathan smiled at him.

"How dare you come into my office with these accusations? Everything you have claimed is a lie. Get the hell out of my office before I drag you out!" Daddy screamed out.

"Before you drag me out of your office, let me refresh your memory."

"Hello, remember me!" the prostitute said to Daddy.

He was stunned and at a loss for words. Then he said, "This is all a lie! *Get* out of my office!"

"Now, that's not nice! You weren't saying that two nights ago," the prostitute argued. "Let me refresh your memory." She pulled out her phone and showed him the video of them engaging in indescribable, uncensored acts.

My nasty, common father, Oliver, was spitting on, tormenting, and whipping her with whips throughout the video. Sadly, I guess that was my father's way of getting his revenge towards the white enemies.

"Turn it off!" Daddy shouted with a tremor in his voice, as he rushed toward her, trying to grab her.

Before he could, Jonathan slammed him into the wall.

"This is what's going to happen. You are going to let my son into this university with that sweet daughter of yours, and you are going to treat him good, you understand? "You still mad that your wife left you and Makira and went with a real boss?" "I made you playboy!" Plus, we both know you weren't hitting that right! Face it; I'm a better man than you will ever be sexually, financially, and physically. I'm the one that makes you shine! If it wasn't for me, you would be another broke black man in jail or on the corner. You will always need me! Just be glad I didn't get to your daughter instead."

Angry, ashamed, hurt, frustrated, and defeated, Daddy came to an agreement. "Get out of my office!" he exclaimed sadly.

"Not until you call my son and tell him that he has the job!" Jonathan demanded. "Now, do it now!" he insisted.

Christian picked up the phone.

"Hello?" he answered.

"Good afternoon. This is Oliver Johnson from Oliver Johnson University. How are you?" Daddy said.

"I'm doing well," Christian said, shocked.

"I was wondering if you were still interested in being an assistant for Miss Makira Johnson?" Daddy said.

"Well, of course I am," Christian said excitedly.

"Great! Can you start tomorrow?"

"*Yes!*" Christian shouted, while he jumped up in the air, overwhelmed. "I promise you won't be sorry!" he yelled and hung up the phone.

"Okay, are you happy? Now go!" Daddy said to Jonathan.

Jonathan and the prostitute smiled as they left Daddy's office.

Discouraged and ashamed, Daddy threw himself in his chair and held his head.

"What have I done?" he said to himself.

He called Christian back and told him to be at the school the following day at nine.

The next day, Sapphire and I were getting ready for the interview we had previously planned for nine that morning. At exactly nine, the interviewee showed up, along with Christian and Daddy.

"You can dismiss this young man because the position has been filled!" Daddy said to me.

"*What?* No, it has not!" I corrected him.

"Yes, it has, and here is your new assistant. I would like you to meet Christian Christiano."

"Have you lost your mind? He is ... He is ..." I said, not finishing my sentence.

Daddy cut me off and repeated, "Your new assistant, Christian Christiano."

"He's *white!*" I blurted out.

"Makira, I am shocked right now! This school is not racist. Now, as I said, the position has been filled!" he said and exited the room.

"So, we meet again. Congratulations!" I said sarcastically to Christian.

"I would say thank you if it wasn't fake," Christian stated with a smile.

"Let's just get to work!" I said as I walked away from him. "What are you looking at?" I yelled out.

"It's hard not to look at you. You are beautiful!" Christian confessed with a smile.

"So, what do you think? Just because you said I'm beautiful and filled me all up, I am supposed to give you some? For your information, I don't need a man to validate what I already know about myself, and if you even think that it takes small words to get in my panties, you are wrong," I explained as I rolled my eyes.

"See, that's what I'm talking about! Can't no man give you a compliment without the second degree. I'm simply just trying to give you props when it is due and talk about us in the future," Christian proclaimed.

"Ha, ha!" I laughed. "That's funny. You really think that I would give you a chance in hot hell? A white man, you?"

"Never say never. Wouldn't want you to eat your own words."

"You are hilarious! Enough, let's get started on this lesson plan so we can get this over with," I announced.

"Fine with me," Christian agreed.

"The lesson plan for this month is about the Harlem Renaissance. The objective is to find a particular individual of this era who impacted you and the phenomenal turnaround for black society."

"Paul Laurence Dunbar! Very smart individual who shined the light on his culture. Speaking on the pros and the cons of being an African American man—" Christian explained.

I cut him off with, "Ha, what you know about being a black man?"

"Oh, Miss Makira, I can too so relate, just in a different shade. I'm at a typically all-black university, with people disqualifying me because of my skin color. There is nothing I can say or do to change anybody's mind or get a fair chance of being treated the same as my peers. Sounds like to me everything is the same," Christian finished.

"It doesn't feel good, does it? You and your ancestors have been doing this to my people for a long time, and it still exists to this day—police shooting at us because we are black, the names we are being called, and the brutality, my ancestors' horrific beatings, the chains, *torture, cries, the rape (males and females), the hangings*! I think you deserve it all!" I said with hatred in my eyes.

"You are so evil!" Christian uttered. "I am sorry for what my ancestors did to your people, but I will not let you call me racist! I love all shades of color. I'm a caring, loving activist, when it comes to any culture's human rights. I favor the African American race the most. When I was little, I had a nanny named Lou, and she was black. I loved that woman with all my heart. She raised me to be the man that I am today," Christian explained. "She taught me everything, including treating all walks of life with dignity and respect. You know what your problem is? You are so quick to judge someone because of what you see on the exterior but don't dare try to see the interior. You want to judge someone, judge yourself. Look in the mirror, and ask yourself, 'Who am I? Why am I still alone?

Why am I a thirty-year-old virgin?'" Christian said as he got up and walked out the door, slamming it behind him.

Let me tell you, it takes a lot to shut me up! He shut me up, y'all!

I just sat there, in silence, crying. After about thirty minutes, I left and went home.

I got home and took a shower! Afterward, I looked at my naked reflection from the exterior to the interior. What I saw in the mirror was a wealthy, well-dressed woman with a smile and encouraging words, but she had second-degree burns and infected scars beneath the skin.

I saw nothing worthwhile.

I called my father to get some encouraging words.

"Hello?" Daddy greeted.

"Hey, Daddy, I just want to know why you hired the snowflake. Were you desperate?" I questioned him.

"Makira, calm down. It's okay to switch it up every now and then," he explained.

"Yeah, right, you don't even like white people period, so what's this really about?" I asked.

"Maybe it's time to give them a fair shot before we start judging them," Daddy testified.

After hearing that garbage, I hung up. I pulled out my diary and started to write what I felt.

Can you teach an old dog new tricks?
Or someone truly changed, try new tricks?
The old is damaged, and the new is recovered
Or is someone old and malicious, wants to keep something covered?

I know my father line by line, inside out! Is my father being blackmailed, forced to do this strange favor to hold a deep, dark secret?

CHAPTER 5

Diagnosis

I tossed and turned in my bed, trying to figure out how and why my father hired a white man—the so-called enemy. Coming up with no other logical reason, I suspected that it was a favor for someone. So I called my father to clear up some questions I had.

Daddy answered, "Good morning, Makira."

"Good morning, Daddy. I have to ask you something," I said.

"Yes, honey, ask me anything," Oliver said.

"You hate white people! I don't understand why you would hire one. You can tell me the truth!" I told him.

"Once again, things can change; people can change. I am hurt that you would come up with these accusations," he responded.

"Father, forgive me, but it's just strange. You told me all my life on this earth to hate the white race and never trust them, and then one day, suddenly everything is fine and dandy? Sorry, Daddy. I'm not buying it!" I refused to accept his answer.

"Well, I don't know what to tell you, my child," he said.

"You can start by telling me the truth!" I shouted.

"Enough, Makira! For the last time, I have changed. Now just shut the hell up!" He slammed the phone down in my ear.

Right then, I definitely knew that my father was hiding something. I sat there and just shook my head. Then I went off to work.

"Good morning, Miss Makira. I made your favorite coffee," Christian said. He smiled as he passed me my coffee mug.

"How could you make my favorite coffee when you don't know how I like my coffee?" I said as I looked at the cup suspiciously.

Christian replied, "Nondecaf, Folgers, six Splenda packages, french vanilla creamer."

Shocked and surprised, I just looked at him and then walked away.

"In the classroom, there are volunteers and students working on the scene for the Harlem Renaissance: *Saturday Nighters* play online.' I'm ready to go over the play scenes," I said.

"Okay," Christian said as he entered my office.

Catching him off guard, I pushed him to the wall and said, "Are you some type of stalker?"

"No," Christian replied.

"Are you trying to wait for the right time and then take advantage of me?" I screamed out.

"No, Makira, relax," Christian said.

"Well, how do you know precisely, down to the measurement, how I like my coffee?" I asked as I stared at him.

"It's called eyes, Makira. I am observant, not just of your physique," he said as he stared at my breasts and hips.

"I followed his eyes and then attempted to slap him, but, quickly, he grabbed my hand and said, "Look, Makira, I have been watching

26

you. Now, excuse me for saying this, but I have this deep crush on you!" He looked me straight in the eyes.

I'm not even going to lie to y'all. I was caught up in my feelings for ten minutes.

Christian tried to move in for the big one, but I quickly woke up from that love spell and smacked him. "Ugh, you are so nasty. Let's get started and stop this red light, green light," I said, walking to my desk to sit down.

Christian took a seat in front of me, rubbing his face.

"I have chosen four students to participate in the Harlem Renaissance play. Eman, writing his profile on himself and Langston Hughes. I love that he interacts with his character and how well he has done on his research on Langston Hughes. I have read things in his profile about Langston Hughes that I would never even have imagined. Langston Hughes was not just battling being an African American. A lot of skeletons were in his closets that he was scared to clear out. Overall, a very good profile," I explained to Christian.

"My second choice is Corey Black, who did a profile of Jean Toomer."

"Another excellent individual in the Harlem Renaissance. I know a lot about this man and his struggle!"

"Kia Mason and Esther Popel."

"Once again, another phenomenal individual! A very religious woman who had set morals and standards."

"Finally, Catrina Askew and Effie Lee Newsome."

"A great woman who participated in the Harlem Renaissance."

"So, Christian, I want you to take these profiles and read over them. Just to get you caught up so you won't be lost. Any questions or concerns?" I asked Christian.

"You have a nice left hand," Christian stated, rubbing his face again.

"I have a nice right too. If you come off like that again, I'll let you find out for yourself," I said. "I'll see you tomorrow for the introduction as my new assistant."

I added, "Stop looking at my butt," as I felt him looking at me.

"It's hard to miss!" Christian replied with a smile.

Blushing, I hurried home and wrote my diary entry: "Can love be black and white?"

CHAPTER 6

Introduction to a New Beginning, Part 1

I washed myself slowly and thoroughly, brushed my hair in the correct posture, and lathered my body with natural oils to get a smooth texture. I locked up my D-cup breasts with an Andres Sarda push-up bra and followed with my special Chanel No. 5 perfume. I decorated my bottom with matching lace boy shorts, followed by a Fendi body-con dress. I grabbed my red bottoms to set off my attire. I looked at the finished product and was very satisfied with what I saw.

"I am a beautiful, strong black woman!" I said to my reflection. I grabbed my designer bag and left the house for work.

Entering the school, I saw there was a fresh pot of my favorite coffee and my favorite apple fritters.

Christian smiled at me and bit his bottom lip. He brought over my coffee and my apple fritter.

"Wow! Good morning! You look amazing!" He looked me up and down.

"Thank you! The students will be here in five minutes. Shall we get started?" I walked past him, smiling, making sure I walked extra hard to have a little jiggle in my behind.

I felt Christian following the patterns of my behind.

"Yes!" he finally responded, mesmerized into a full trance. "Excuse me if I am out of line, but, once again, you look very nice today. What is the occasion?" Christian said, getting closer.

"There is no occasion; I always look this way," I said.

"Well, indeed you do, but, uuhh ..." he said as he scooted closer to me, rubbing on my thighs. "You look extra good today. You know what you are doing with that tight dress and them breasts sitting up like that. You know I'm looking," he added, still rubbing on my thighs.

He got close to my ear and whispered, "It takes a real man to handle all this," as he licked my earlobe.

So at this point, I was really feeling this type of action! Cold chills ran up my spine at his intense sexual glare. We started to meet each other at the midline, but suddenly, the students began entering the classroom.

"Good morning!" I said, quickly getting myself together.

"Good morning!" all the students said.

"What's going on in here, and who is this?" Eman said.

"I'll let you know in a second," I answered. "Can I help you?" I said to an unusual person I had never seen before with baggy clothes and this ugly gray hat.

The person lifted her head and said, "It's me, Kia."

I looked at Kia and saw every bruise and punch mark on her.

"What happened to you? You're bruised up, and you're wearing baggy clothes and that ugly gray hat? What's going on?" I said.

Kia walked away from me and took her seat in a daze.

See, Kieron, Kia's boyfriend and baby's father was a petty drug dealer and control freak. The night before, he had been arrested for drinking in public and disturbing the peace. The good woman Kia was, she went and bailed him out with the money she had been saving for a rainy day.

Now check this out! This arrogant punk could only tell her, "You know you are nothing without me," as he staggered out of the jail cell.

Kia replied, "I know!" as she drove them home.

After running into the wall twice and tripping, face-first, to the sidewalk, he finally reached the front door.

He went to the kitchen to get a bottle of vodka.

Kia sadly looked at him and said, "Baby, please put it down!" Kia tried to take the alcohol out of his hand.

"Move, b——h!" he said as he took the bottle of vodka and broke it with a hit to Kia's head.

Kia fell unconscious to the ground. Kieron started to hit her repeatedly until his hand got tired. Then, he pulled a big chunk of Kia's hair out of her scalp!

She was in a daze. Forty minutes later, all she heard was huffing and puffing in her ear. Sweat dripped down her face.

When she finally opened her eyes, it was to rape. Terrified, she turned her head until he finished. Kieron finished up and bit her cheek, leaving a bite mark on her face as he rolled off of her.

"You got some good stuff down there!" Kieron said.

Kia looked out the window across the classroom, and a tear fell out of her eye as she came out of her daze. Kia hurried to catch the tears that tried to escape and participate in class.

"Once again, good morning, class," I said. "First and foremost, I would like to say that everyone did an awesome job with their profiles, and—trust me—it was very hard to choose just four students to participate in the play: Eman Jafar as Langston Hughes, Kia Mason as Esther Popel, Catrina Askew as Effie Lee Lawson, and Corey Black as Jean Toomer. Congratulations to everyone!"

"Who is this white guy?" Eman Jafar asked again.

"Yeah, yeah, yeah!" all the other students said as Sapphire entered the room and took her seat.

"All right, everyone calm down," I said to the students. "This mysterious white man is Christian Christiano, and he was appointed by Mr. Oliver Johnson to be my new assistant professor until Sapphire comes back," I announced.

"*Aaawww helll naw*! What does a white man know about black history?" Eman Jafar said angrily.

"Nothing!" Corey Black said. "Man, your daddy must've had his eyes closed when he said yes to this."

"Now wait a minute, class," Sapphire said out loud. "Just because Mr. Christian is a Caucasian man doesn't mean that he is ignorant of the African American culture and heritage," she said, standing up.

"Oh yeah, my bad. He does know about our heritage." "He knew what size whip to whip us with." Corey Black said.

All his classmates came to an agreement with him.

"Enough!" I shouted out. "Now, I hate this as much as you do, but Mr. Oliver Johnson says it is for the best."

"Well, no disrespect, Ms. Makira, but when I first came in the classroom, it looked as though you and the white man was getting a little close," Corey blurted out.

"Look, Corey, you are getting way out of hand. Now, if you don't want me to change my mind about your grade, you better shut up and sit down!" I said.

"That's blackmail," Corey said.

"I don't care. Sit down," I demanded.

Christian stood up and said, "Look, I think it is preposterous for all of you to judge me because of my skin color! I am not the enemy. If you get to know me, you'll see I am really down to earth. Never judge a book by its cover!" Christian announced.

They all smacked their teeth and rolled their eyes. The bell rang, and the students exited the classroom.

"Make sure that the four students who are participating in the play rehearse their profiles. Thank you!" I said.

"What type of person are you? You and the students were very obnoxious and downright ignorant to Christian. What's your problem? It's just not human for you to act this way!" Sapphire yelled.

"Don't forget what color you are, Sapphire," I reminded her. "Do you think Mr. Christian here would give you a job at his establishment if he had one?" I yelled at her.

"Do you think if your father was not the founder of this establishment you would have a chance to be who you are today?" Sapphire replied.

I lifted my hand to smack Sapphire, and she grabbed my hand and said, "The truth hurts, don't it?"

I snatched my hand away from Sapphire and just looked at her.

Angrily, Sapphire left the classroom and slammed the door.

"Wow, so I don't feel that bad now. I'm not the only one you want to smack! Look, we both are having a bad day. You and your students want to lynch me, and you and Sapphire want to have a slap fest. Why don't we go chill at the Jazz Bistro on Thirteenth Street?" Christian asked.

"Am I hearing this correctly? I treat you like the scum of the earth, and you want to take me out for a drink?" I said.

"Well, you can't help it that you are in between yourself and don't know how to follow your own heart. So how can you know how to treat me?" Christian explained.

"You don't know what you are talking about!" I clarified madly.

"Yeah, I know! Come on; let's just relax with each other. It's been a long day," Christian confirmed.

"No, thank you! I know what a harmless drink can do. Yeah, I'll pass," I said, loading up my briefcase.

"You are impossible sometimes!" Christian exclaimed. "Well, if you change your mind, I'll be there," Christian finished as he left the classroom.

"I'm going home!" I confirmed to myself. I grabbed my things and left the classroom.

In the car, I tried to drown my thoughts of Christian with some Erykah Badu music, but I couldn't.

"I am kind of thirsty. It won't hurt to have one little drink."

I turned my car around to go to the Jazz Bistro club. Ten minutes later, I arrived at the Jazz Bistro club and sat at the bar. I ordered a bloody Mary and listened to the beautiful sounds of jazz music.

Five minutes later, Christian spotted me out and sent over a Long Island iced tea.

The bartender said to me, "Compliments of the man at the table to your left," handing me the drink.

I took the drink and said, "Thank you!"

"He wants you to come sit with him," the bartender said.

"Thank you again," I said.

"He is really hot!" the bartender said to me.

I smiled at the bartender and walked to the table where Christian sat.

"Thank you for the drink!" I greeted him.

"You're welcome!" Christian said as he looked me up and down.

"I have a question about your culture," I said to Christian.

"Ask away!" Christian told me.

"Okay, thank God you don't fit this criteria: Why does white people's breath smell like salami?"

"Wow, I don't even know how to respond. Well, ummm, we do like salami, and sometimes the smell may kinda stick to us!"

"No harm in that," I replied.

We laughed together.

"Well, since we are asking each other about our cultures, my question to you is why don't African American people smile in their pictures, and why can't some African Americans swim?" Christian questioned.

"It's a pride thing! We don't want to show any emotion because we are mysterious, strong, and can conquer all. "Deep water is not our thing." Have you ever dated a black woman, Christian?"

"Well, first, before answering your question, I was like you, dating my own culture because I knew that people would accept me, but I always *loved* me some black women. Yes, to answer your question. Her name was Amber Carrington, and I was truly in love with her. She was my everything. We eloped and married at the justice of the peace because we knew that her parents would not accept this marriage. We both wanted kids, but before we could, she died in a horrible car crash. That was four years ago," Christian said, teary-eyed. "I loved that woman with all my heart," he sadly finished.

The tears began to form, piling up on each other. I saw it and said, "Hey, let's dance! Hopefully you can stay on beat, 'cause you know y'all can't dance!"

"Haha!" Christian said as he grabbed my hand.

My favorite Erykah Badu song, "Next Lifetime," played in the background. As we entered the dance floor, holding each other, we looked deeply into each other's soul. We weren't moving too fast or too slow! Everything was perfect.

"Dang, y'all, white boy got game!"

"You know, something good can be right in front of your face," Christian stated.

"I know, and it scares me," I confessed.

Things were getting hot and heavy—like, soon he was about to get the business, if you know what I mean! So I started putting the moves on him!

Real close and personal, I gave him a wet whisper in his ear, "You can touch it; I know you want to."

"Mmm, don't play with me like that! You know I want to," Christian testified, getting aroused.

Roughly, I grabbed Christian's hands and placed them firmly on my behind. "This is where they are supposed to be!" I licked Christian's earlobe.

"I knew that you wanted me the way I wanted you!" he said as he lifted my behind with his hands.

"Some secrets are best left unsaid!" I said with a smile.

CHAPTER 7

Introduction to a New Beginning—Part 2

Now, before I get into Kia's crazy man and the trials and tribulations she had to go through with him, I know y'all want a little visual of how she looks. Well, picture it, Sicily 1960! I'm playing! Kia is a dark-chocolate, almond-brown-eyed, four-foot-ten-inch woman with a Georgia-peaches booty, thick thighs, a little stomach from her last child, and the stretch marks—you know, the oatmeal pie stomach! She has a beautiful heart-shaped face with juicy, luscious lips and a Cabbage Patch–doll nose with a hoop nose ring.

She is my favorite student because her swag is off the charts and because she has a unique mind-set, is very creative, and has a funny personality. I absolutely love this girl!

Anyway, after school, Kia got a phone call from her children's school stating that Kieron didn't pick up their son, King.

Kia answered the phone, and the teacher said, "Hello! This is King's teacher, Mary Scott. I have King with me once again because your husband forgot to pick him up. Miss Kia, we can't keep having this happen!" Mary shouted.

"I'm so sorry. I'll be right there," Kia said and got off the phone.

Kia arrived fifteen minutes later at the school.

"I'm sorry once again! This will not happen again," Kia said, pleadingly.

"It better not! I'm starting to think that you are incapable of taking care of these kids," Mary Scott said as she rolled her eyes and went back into the school.

Kia tried so hard to hold back her tears.

"Why didn't Daddy pick me up?" King asked his mother.

"Daddy just forgot, baby; that's all," Kia stated.

"Okay!" King said excitedly.

Kia began to cry because she knew the reason why Kieron didn't pick him up.

When she got home, she confronted Kieron about his behavior.

"Why didn't you pick King up as well?" Kia shouted.

"Cause he ain't my son." He kissed their daughter Kiora's cheek.

"Mommy, I thought you said Daddy forgot," King said sadly.

"Baby, go into your room and start your homework," Kia said.

"You can't treat him like that, Kieron!" Kia yelled out.

"Man, what are you talking about? He is not my son," Kieron said as he brushed Kia off.

"Kieron, I haven't been with no one else except you," Kia assured him.

"It's not my f——n' son! I don't make retarded babies. Look at him making retarded noises! Always jumping up and down like he is retarded!" Kieron yelled.

"How dare you say that? He is autistic! That doesn't make him retarded! You know what, the one I think is retarded is you!" Kia screamed out.

Kieron was so furious that he kicked Kia down, got on top of her, and started punching her in the face.

Kiora jumped up and started hitting her father, Kieron, on the back, and King started punching him in the head.

Kieron got extremely upset, so upset that he pulled out a gun and shot King in the back.

Now, outside, Kieron's boss, Beenie, and Samuel, also known as the "Ghost Sniper" (the hitman for Beenie), heard the gunshot!

Now, I'm going to stop for a second right here and get you caught up on these two cats!

Beenie is a six-foot-tall, broad-cut, muscular albino man with a glass eye and a light-grey eye and red facial hair. He always got bullied by his peers about his skin complexion. They said he looked like a "bleach spot," and the girls thought he had a disease because of his complexion. He became a drug dealer for the money, power, and respect!

Samuel is a Russian native. He is six-foot-five and very built with blond hair and blue eyes. He was an orphan in Russia. Growing up, he always had to fight for everything! In the shelter, everyone became afraid of him, and because of this reputation, the Russian system took him and made him a sniper! Samuel wanted out, so they tried to kill him, but he killed them. Samuel fled to the United States in a dead man's casket and changed his identity!

The two met and became "Clyde and Clyde of Mississippi."

Back to the story—quickly, they hurried and busted down the door.

Samuel saw Kieron on top of Kia, beating the sense out of her.

Without hesitation, he went over to Kieron and pulled him off of Kia, punching him like lightning, left and right. Blood was flying everywhere.

"I need him to live, Ghost," Beenie said as he took Kiora and King to the car.

Samuel kicked Kieron for the last time and then picked Kia up. He got in the car with Beenie, and they drove to the hospital.

Samuel held Kia's unconscious body, silently looking at her. The doctors started emergency surgery on King to remove the bullet embedded in his spine.

Samuel went back and forth from Kia's room to King's room.

Because Kia was still out of it, the doctor told him that King would never walk again! Samuel showed no emotion, but, inside, he felt remorse for King.

"Ghost, they'll stay at my house with my grandma. We will deal with that fool later," Beenie said to Samuel.

A week later, Kia and King were discharged from the hospital and Kia and her two children went to live with Beenie.

"I'm gonna let y'all stay here for a while," Beenie said to Kia and the kids. "I just need you to take care of my grandmother, and I will pay you. I don't usually do this for anyone, but I see you are going through a hard time, and you shouldn't. You're welcome to everything in this house, but don't go into the basement. You understand?" Beenie said seriously.

"Yes," Kia answered.

Beenie walked out of the room, and Samuel walked in. He just rubbed the side of Kia's face with no sound.

"You ready, Ghost?" Beenie said.

Samuel walked out of the room and proceeded to the car with Beenie. They went to the block where Kieron was.

"What's up, boss man?" Kieron yelled to Beenie as he went to the car window.

"Get in the car, fool," Beenie said to Kieron.

Kieron got in the car, and they all drove to the safe spot.

"What the hell is your problem, fool? Why you beat up your girl like that?" Beenie said to Kieron.

"She got smart, so I had to put her in check! That's not my son," Kieron explained.

"You know what? You are one ignorant mutha f——a," Beenie said to Kieron.

"Man forget all that! Where is she at 'cause I'm horny," Kieron replied, holding his crotch area."

You lucky I like my bait dead; otherwise, I would definitely give you a run for your money."

Now, let me pause right here and get y'all caught up. "This man got some serious insecure issues! He tried numerous times to get women's attention but always got rejected, which he hated. Dead people can't talk!" But back to the story.

"When you gon' give her back to me since you ain't interested," Kieron asked.

"You ain't getting her back. You don't know how to treat her," Beenie said.

"Now, go out there and make me some money," Beenie said.

"Watch that fool and make sure he ain't doing nothing out the way. I don't trust him."

Samuel left and went to watch Kieron.

So furious with Beenie, Kieron went to Beenie's twin brother, Rage, Beenie's archenemy, to sell some of Beenie's products to him.

Okay, Rage is a drug dealer too, but not as good as Beenie. No, no! Rumor has it, one taste of Beenie's product will have you hooked for *life*!

Beenie and Rage are fraternal twins. Beenie is Albino African American and Rage is dark-skinned African American. Ever since they were in their mother's womb, they fought constantly. The hatred they share for each other is indescribable.

Now, this is the kicker here! One of the weirdest things I don't understand is, no matter what, they will fight for each other if someone else takes advantage of them. It's crazy but anyway …

"What's up, Rage?" Kieron said. "I have something for you! Me and your brother ain't seeing eye to eye right now."

Kieron threw the heroin to Rage. Deep down, Rage knew that his brother's product was better than his. Rage smelled it and tasted it.

"How you going to try to sell me my brother's sh——t?" Rage asked Kieron.

"Like I said, we are not seeing eye to eye right now," Kieron stated again. "So, is we like partners or not?"

Rage started to smile and asked his right-hand man, "You hear this dude?"

They both started to laugh, and Rage got up and approached Kieron.

Quickly, he hit him in the head with his gun, knocking him clean out! "The second thing I hate on this earth is a traitor. I hate my brother, but I respect him. Take him back to Beenie!" Rage taped a sign on Kieron's head that said "Traitor" with Beenie's product.

Beenie came to the door and saw Kieron with the note attached to his forehead.

Kia heard the knock at the door as well and came to the top of the stairway to see who it was. Struggling to see who was there, she just started to listen.

"Dumb fool!" Beenie dragged his body into the house to the dungeon.

42

Beenie called Samuel, "Hey, I need you to come and take out the trash."

Samuel listened and hung up the phone. Ten minutes later, he came into the house and entered Beenie's dungeon.

He saw Kieron's limbs cut off, lying on the floor, and heard his screams of agony.

Kia ran back to the bedroom and started crying.

Samuel heard footsteps and proceeded to the door. Pulling out his gun, he started up the stairs.

Kia covered her head, scared to death.

Samuel proceeded into the bedroom and walked to the bed. He got in the bed with her and just held her.

Kia cried loudly until she fell asleep.

In the morning, Beenie came to find Samuel and Kia lying in the bed together. He smiled and shut the door.

King rolled his wheelchair into the room with his mother and Samuel.

"What did you do to my mom?" King asked.

Samuel finally spoke for the first time in four years with his Russian accent. He said happily, "Nothing! She's sleeping. Do you want something to eat?"

"Yes!" King said excitedly.

Samuel went and got Kiora from the other room and proceeded downstairs to fix the children breakfast.

Kia finally got up and went to the room where her kids were, but they were not there. She yelled their names as she ran down the stairs.

"Good morning, Mommy!" King and Kiora said.

Kia smiled and looked at Samuel.

"Thank you!" she said.

Samuel looked up at Kia and agreed with a nod. Beenie entered the kitchen. He smacked Kia's buttocks and kissed her cheek. Kia turned her face and looked at him.

"Good morning, everyone!" Beenie said as Samuel stared at him with anger.

The tension was high. Beenie sat in front of Samuel and just smiled.

"Let's go get cleaned up and go outside," Kia said to the kids.

"Yay!" they said.

Beenie and Samuel looked at each other.

"I need you to stay focused! You don't need no distraction. Leave her alone!" Beenie said.

Samuel left the kitchen and went outside to play with Kia's kids.

Kia saw how good Samuel was with the kids and became very attracted to him.

Samuel had his eyes closed, playing hide-and-seek with the kids.

Kia walked over to Samuel and kissed his cheek. He stopped counting and looked at Kia. She smiled and walked away.

Samuel watched her as she walked into the house. He then saw Beenie in the window, looking angry.

Later that day, Kia, suspecting that Beenie was up to no good, took the money he had been giving her, plus Kieron's hidden stash, and used it to get out of Beenie's house before things got too crazy. She packed and at noon tried to leave the house with her kids.

When they got downstairs, Beenie asked her, "Where do you think you're going?"

Scared to death, Kia replied, "I thank you for letting me stay here, but I think it's best for me to leave."

"You're not going nowhere," Beenie said. "You know, I would love for you to be one of my projects." He walked toward Kia and pushed her bag out of her hand.

Boom! Samuel flew in like a firecracker, jumped over the coach, and slammed Beenie to the floor. They began to fight.

Kia took the kids and ran far away.

Back and forth, Beenie and Samuel fought. It was a very close fight, until Samuel picked Beenie up off the floor and started punching him in the face, breaking his nose and other facial bones. He stopped punching him when he saw he wasn't breathing.

Beenie's grandmother was screaming at the top of the stairway.

Samuel blacked-out, possessed by numerous evil spirits, walked up the stairs as she ran. His eyes got blacker as he shot her multiple times.

He grabbed the bodies and disposed of them in his secret hideout.

Afterward, he went back to his house and sat down with a beer in his hand.

Drunk after eight beers, he stared at all the people he had killed in the room. Finally, he fell into a drunk sleep and dreamed.

There was a voice at the water with forgiveness! It was bright; the water was sparkling. The wind went through his hair as if it were embracing him. He then saw a man at the altar. He jumped up, rubbed his eyes, got himself together, and left his house.

He drove to the water.

The same voice from his dream embraced him and said, "Turn from your wicked ways!"

Tears fell from his face as he got back into the car and drove to the church he had seen in his dream.

When he got out of the car, he felt evil spirits pulling him back, screaming. He fought his way into the church.

It got so severe he had to crawl into the church. There were so many black shadows screaming and running out of Samuel. Samuel became so weak that he fell to the altar in front of the pastor. A new life had begun.

CHAPTER 8

Lovers' Lane

I woke up from a beautiful slumber.

The rays of the sun were shining brighter than ever. I got up and beautified myself for a new horizon, wearing a navy-blue body-con dress, a silver diamond necklace, and silver pumps. I was the bomb. com! Off I went to work.

As usual, when I got to work, Christian had my coffee and apple fritter waiting for me.

"Thank you again, Christian," I said with a smile.

"Again, Makira, it is my pleasure," Christian said and smiled at me.

The students entered the classroom, and the staff who did the recording started to get in place.

Five minutes later, the camera guy instructed them to get in their places and said that they would be rolling in "Three, two …"

"Good morning, class and online viewers. Today, I will be announcing our new play: *The Harlem Renaissance Presents the*

Saturday Nighters. The play takes place in a club in Harlem. This is a club where we, the Harlem Renaissance participants, come to express our thoughts on literature and common situations and give one another encouraging words and food for thought. I have chosen four students out of my class to participate in this play. As I call your name, please stand up and let everyone know who your character is and why you chose him or her. Corey Black!"

"Hello. My name is Corey Black, and my profile is about Jean Toomer. I chose Jean Toomer because he spoke, in my opinion, about the true struggle of a black man."

"Thank you, Corey. Next, Eman Jafar."

"Hello, I am Eman Jafar, and my profile is on Langston Hughes. I chose Langston Hughes because his work is one word—*promiscuous!*"

"Wow, that is a good word to sum a person up. Thank you!" I said.

"Hello, my name is Kia Mason, and my profile is on Esther Popel. I chose Esther Popel because she is like me, a conservative individual who teaches and exercises her religious beliefs in and out of her work," Kia said and sat down.

"Excellent!" I said. "And last but not least, Catrina Askew."

"Hello to all. My name, as stated, is Catrina Askew, and I am honored to play the role of Effie Lee Lawson. I chose Effie Lee Lawson because she stood up tall and kept her head held high for her culture. She embraced and endured any speculation that came forth because of her nationality."

"Awesome! I can't wait to see each and every one of you in action," I concluded. "Each student has thirty minutes to thoroughly discuss their profile in depth. The performance should be clear, crisp, and appetizing. Each performance includes a major score. So, your performance means everything! Until next time, students and live audience, have a good day, and get ready for *The Saturday Nighters.* Next time, it will be the play, so make sure you are studying your profile. Class is dismissed!" I released them.

"Wow, I'm ready! I want to express myself," Christian said, smiling.

"Well, class is over, so express yourself out the door," I said, looking at him funny.

"Hahaha! Look—I meant it; I want to recite some poetry. Why don't we head down to the Soul Wired Café," Christian suggested.

"First of all, what do you know about poetry, and second of all, no, I am vanished!" I exclaimed.

"Well, if you change your mind, I will be there," Christian said as he left the room.

I rolled my eyes and went back to what I was doing.

Driving home, I started to think about Christian's invitation and said to myself, "Well, it's not like I have anything else to do at home, and I am kind of hungry. I should just go."

Turning my car around, I proceeded to the café where Christian was.

After forty-five minutes, I arrived at the Soul Wired Café. Going in, I looked around diligently for Christian.

Finally, I spotted him sticking out like a sore thumb and then proceeded to the bar. I couldn't look desperate, y'all, and let him win. Yes! I'm a little childish! I played as if I didn't see him.

Christian saw me at the bar. I know because I saw him with my peripheral vision, and he smiled. Now, usually, he would send someone, like the waitress, over to get me, but I guess, hipped to my game, he took another approach. So, I played the game too, but wait a minute! Check this out! Another black woman who went to college with him, an old friend, He greeted her.

"Brittany, is that you?" Christian asked.

"Christian!" Brittany responded. "Oh my God! It's been some years! Come here, Christian!" She hugged him.

I watched from across the room, wondering why the hell Christian was talking to this girl. I put my drink to my lips to take a sip but felt nauseous and threw it into a nearby garbage can instead.

"How have you been doing, Christian?" Brittany asked.

"I've been doing fine. I have recently gotten a new job at Oliver Johnson University as an assistant to a professor," Christian explained.

"Isn't that school with only black people?" Brittany asked.

"Well, yes!" Christian stated.

"Don't you feel a little different?" Brittany asked.

"They want me to, but at the end of the day, we are all people with red blood running through our veins."

I know that Christian was feeding on my emotions because he quickly glanced over at me with a little smirk on his face.

Christian then grabbed Brittany's hand and smiled at her. That was it for me!

Where is my Vaseline and Timberland boots—because I was about to stomp a mudhole in this chick! Honey child was going down!

I got up and proceeded to the table where they were. I heard Christian ask Brittany, "Have you found anyone yet?"

Extremely furious, I interrupted, "I don't know about Miss Brittany, but you have, Christian! Who is this two-dollar ho?" I asked.

"My name is Brittany, and it is nice to meet you!" she said to me.

"Not for me it isn't!" I replied.

"Well, ummm, Christian, it was nice to see you again," she said as she left.

"Who was that, Christian?" I asked.

"She's just a friend," he explained.

"What type of friend—a friend with benefits or just a friend?" I asked.

I held my hip, still looking at Christian like I could kill him for even daring to look at another woman.

"Look, Makira, she's just a friend, one of my college friends; that's it. Now can you please sit down!" Christian said.

"You don't own me! I'll sit down when I'm good and ready," I said as I lifted my head up in the air.

"Fine. You keep standing there."

Finally, after five minutes, my feet started to get tired, so I sat down.

"Wow!" Christian smiled.

"Shut up. You don't tell me what to do," I said, rolling my eyes.

"On that note, what's your favorite food?" Christian asked me.

"Pork chops smothered in gravy, extra onions, and mashed potatoes," I said. "And yours, Christian?"

"Lasagna with garlic bread and a chef-tossed salad," Christian answered.

"Mmm, that's one of my favorite meals. What's your favorite color?" I asked.

"Green," Christian responded.

"Why green?" I asked.

"Because green shows a sign of riches and fulfillment to me," Christian explained. "What's your favorite color, Makira?"

"Orange," I replied.

"Why orange?" Christian questioned.

"Because of its boldness; it's vibrant and soothing," I said.

"Wow, okay, what's a couple of things you like to do in your spare time?" Christian asked.

"I like to listen to jazz or some Erykah Badu and write some poetry or paint," I replied. "And you, Christian?"

"I like to write poetry and go sailing, fishing, hiking, camping, rock climbing, and surfing," Christian responded.

"You're very adventurous and spontaneous, I see!"

"Yes. I'm very spontaneous," Christian added.

"I like spontaneous," I said.

"How spontaneous?" Christian asked with a smile.

"What are you about to do?"

Christian got up and walked toward the stage.

"Oh my God!" I said, scared to death.

"I have a poem I have written for this special person in my life. See, this person feels the same way about me but has a hard time expressing her feelings, but I don't. Here it is, my poem dedicated to her, my plus one, my everything, my secret admirer. Oh yeah, by the way, my love, I did come prepared with this poem because I knew that you would come tonight!" Christian exclaimed.

"Oh my God! That's my baby, y'all!"

"This poem is called 'My Sweet Secret,' and it goes like this:

My Sweet Secret
If this is a spell, I never want to wake up.
Mmmm, thinking about the outline of your figure when you walk,
How everything moves in slow motion,
The reflection of your honey-nut eyes reflecting off mine.
Ohhhh, the way they play mysterious disguises.
I know you want me the way I want you.
You don't have to be afraid or even scared;
If you confide in me and leave your mind in a slumber,
I promise you I won't tell!"

The crowd, including me, gave Christian a standing ovation.

"That was beautiful!" I declared.

"Not as nearly as beautiful as you!" Christian said.

"You want to leave now? It's about closing time in ten minutes anyways," I suggested.

"Yeah, that's fine. I'll walk you to your car," Christian stated.

"Thank you," I said as I walked out the door. "I had a really good time tonight, Christian!" I blushed.

"I always have a good time when I'm around you, Makira," Christian said as he lifted my head up, looking into my eyes. "Remember that thing you said you like about being spontaneous?" he said as he got closer to my face, roughly around the lip area.

"I'm already ahead of you," I said as I grabbed Christian's face and laid a big tongue-tying kiss on him.

I'm thinking to myself, *His tongue game is on point! Imagine what else he can do with his tongue! Lord, I shouldn't be thinking like this!*

It got extremely hot and heavy. I gently put my finger over his lips, because it was too early to give up the puna!

"I'll see you tomorrow in school!" I said and kissed him softly.

He opened the door for me, and I drove off.

I got home and jumped up and down. I was so excited, y'all.

I hurried and got into something suitable for bed. I reached into my nightstand for my diary and wrote, "I have entered into Lovers' Lane!"

CHAPTER 9

Lovers' Lane Part 2

After the death of Kieron, Kia had started dating prematurely and having sex with numerous men, trying to find true love. Hitting a brick wall, she finally realized that she was going about it the wrong way and changed her ways quickly. Kia turned her life around and started faithfully going to church, living a humble, faith-filled life.

Kia gave her cares, her all, herself, to God. She did not want a man—well, let me scratch that, a *boy*—who didn't respect himself or her to beat her, verbally abuse her, and downgrade her as a chick on the corner.

She wanted a man, a man who would accept her and her kids, someone who would love her unconditionally! I'm talking through her past mistakes, the stretch marks and saggy titties from childbirth, the undesirable baby fat that is so hard to get rid of, you name it— her true Boaz!

Life for her had gotten so much better. She got two jobs at the church—bookstore attendant and choir member. Her recipe for success was that she tithed frequently and stayed focused on God!

It was Friday Night, and it was the healing and deliverance service. Kia was singing in the choir. The service was so anointed that night. Left and right, people of the church were getting their breakthroughs!

Kia dropped to her knees on stage and just went for broke, giving thanks to the Almighty God—thanks that God had removed her from her past situations, thanks that even if no one else thought she was pretty, God did. Despite her imperfections, God felt she was perfect! She knew that it could have been worse—her son could be dead, but he was alive. She believed that her son would walk again, despite what the doctor said!

Pastor turned and looked at King in the audience. He walked up to King and smiled at him, as he knew the great things God had planned for him that night! Kia started rejoicing and crying out ahead of time, because she was in faith and had trust in the Lord her son would walk again.

"Jesus, Jesus, Jesus!" Kia cried out.

Pastor said to King, "Do you believe that you will walk again?"

King, excited, said, "Yes, yes, I can!"

"Well, walk, walk, my son!" Pastor yelled out.

King struggled getting out of the chair! He fell to the ground and walked on his hands, dragging his legs on the floor and then crawling, which led to walking!

The whole congregation screamed with praise and rejoicing.

Kia ran off the stage and hugged him tight.

Touched and moved, Samuel came to the altar and wrapped his arms around Kia and King.

Pastor, excited, said, "This is a picture of your new beginning, Samuel."

After church, Kia went to Samuel and said, "I didn't know that you attended this church."

"I know," Samuel responded.

"I know that you are a man of few words, so I'm just going to cut to the chase. Would you like to attend the singles date night with me?" Kia questioned him.

Samuel paused and nodded his head in agreement.

"Okay, I'll see you tomorrow," Kia stated.

The next day, all the singles went to the movies. Kia made sure that she was dressed to impress. Samuel picked her up, and they went to the movies.

Samuel, stunned, greeted Kia and told her, "You look beautiful."

"Thank you!" Kia responded. "It's been a long time since I heard those words."

Kia wrapped her arm around him, and they walked side by side into the movies.

After the movies, they went to the water where Samuel had heard the voice of God.

"I want to be a better man for myself and you," he said as he turned and looked at Kia. "The first time I laid eyes on you, I knew I loved you, and from what I remember, I never loved anybody," Samuel confessed to Kia.

"Why didn't you say anything?" Kia asked.

"Wasn't the right time. Everything has its own season," Samuel finished.

Kia cried and kissed him on his lips.

Samuel just sat there, not knowing what was going on or how to react. He gently pushed her back and asked Kia, "Are you ready to go?"

Confused, Kia said, "I guess so on that note!"

The ride home was silent.

Kia started smelling her breath to see if it was that, but she didn't smell anything out of the ordinary.

"It's not your breath," Samuel said.

"Well, what's wrong?" Kia asked.

Just in time, he pulled up to Kia's new apartment.

"Have a good night," Samuel said.

"Wow, you're not going to walk me to my door?" she asked.

"For what?" Samuel questioned Kia.

Kia just looked at Samuel for a second and then got out of the car.

Samuel hurried behind her and said, "Wait a minute! Look, the truth is, all I know how to do is kill. I don't know anything about walking you to the door or any other things about dating or dates. Please forgive me," he apologized.

"Well, why you didn't tell me? I was a little offended at first, but I see why now. Come in," Kia said, grabbing his hand.

"If you ever feel uncomfortable about anything, let me know and we can work on it together," she assured Samuel.

"Can we try kissing again?" Samuel suggested.

Kia smiled and said, "Okay! Just relax, and I'll lead."

She grabbed Samuel's hand and started kissing him nice and slow.

Samuel started to follow her lead and rubbed her face. She stopped and kissed his hands; then she moved back to kissing his lips.

Hot and bothered, he stopped and said, "I feel funny. Should we stop?"

"Yes! We should stop before we go any further!" Kia explained.

Samuel agreed and went home.

The next singles night out was a 1970s-themed night out at the skating rink. Kia dressed up with her bell bottoms and Afro puffs, while Samuel came as himself.

Kia went up to him and asked him, "Would you like to dance?"

Samuel smiled for the first time.

"Wow! I don't know if that is for me or my crazy outfit," Kia explained.

"Both!" Samuel said.

They both went to the dance floor. Samuel and Kia moved slowly as their bodies melted on each other. Samuel held Kia tightly as he kissed on her neck. The tension was there. With his manhood stern and alert, he started going down Kia's panties.

Kia hurried and stopped him. She said, "Not here. Let's go home!"

So they both returned their skates and left.

In the car, Samuel started to rub on Kia, as Kia did the same to him. At every stoplight, they started to kiss passionately.

When they got into the house, they were like animals after fresh meat. The foreplay began from the hickies on the neck to the heavy breathing in the ear to Samuel's shirt coming off.

Gathering herself together, Kia said, "We will call it a night. Having premarital sex doesn't do anything but mess things up."

Samuel genuinely accepted her wishes and went home.

When he got home, all he could do was think about Kia. He laid in his bed and imagined Kia beside him, naked, rubbing on his chest, about to kiss him, and then the phone rang.

Pastor had called to check on him.

Samuel answered.

"Hey, Samuel, is everything okay with you?" Pastor asked.

"I want to marry her! I know that she is the one!" Samuel stated.

"Do you think that it's too soon?" Pastor questioned.

"No, it is just right!" he exclaimed. "Our next date, I want to pop the question!"

"Well, if you are sure, then it's fine with me," Pastor responded.

In the meantime, days turned into weeks and weeks turned into months!

Samuel and Kia talked on the phone about life goals, making love, ethnic backgrounds, children, hurt, pain, love, and interests. Finally, it was time for that next date!

Samuel took Kia on their final date, where he would pop the big question.

He led Kia to a beautiful decorated area in the forest. It was an isolated, secured space, surrounded with trees and white doves. There were pure white roses on the ground around a big white canopy bed with canopy lights and sheer, shimmery curtains.

"Why are we in the forest?" Kia asked.

"It's a surprise," Samuel replied.

They both went into the beautiful lit area with the doves and white roses. A man was standing there dressed in white.

Kia, shocked, said, "Oh my God!" holding her mouth.

Samuel got in front of Kia and got on one knee. "Kia, I've never had this type of feeling for anyone. You have made me become a better man. Proverbs 18:22 says, 'He who finds a wife finds a good thing and obtains favor from the Lord!' I thought I would never change, let alone that God would send someone as precious as you! I would love to spend the rest of my life with you forever and ever. Would you do me the honors of being my wife?" Samuel proposed.

Lost for words and shocked, Kia accepted his proposal.

Pastor congratulated the two and started the wedding ceremony. Afterward, the pastor left them alone.

Samuel looked deep into Kia's eyes and started kissing her.

Kia anxiously removed Samuel's clothing, and he removed hers, but when Samuel got to taking off her top garments, she held her bra and put her face down. Kia was very self-conscious of her oatmeal pie stomach and titties because Kieron use to joke that her titties were saggy and separated. One hung to the right and the other to the left!

"I love you for you!" Samuel said as he kept undressing her and embracing her.

Gently, Kia pushed Samuel onto the bed and covered his naked body with hers. From the top of his forehead down to his pinkie toe, she pleasured him.

Now, you know what they say about white men and their private parts—well, that didn't apply to crazy Mr. Russian man! From what Kia said, Mr. Russian was packing 9 men strong! Ain't no way, but to each its own!

Kia cried out from the pain and pleasure.
One hour later, both bodies trembled in ecstasy.
Kia laid there, restless, on Samuel.
Samuel looked down at Kia and said, "I love you!"
"I love you too," Kia said.

CHAPTER 10

Caught in the Rapture of Love

I woke up with a smile on my face and a new pep in my step—out with old and in with the new! Very excited, I covered my figure with one of my favorite snug dresses and complemented it with red-bottom heels, of course.

I grabbed my briefcase and my Michael Kors handbag and proceeded out the door for work.

Once again, Christian was the first one to meet and greet me; usually, it would be with my apple fritter and coffee but not that morning. No, that particular Friday, it was more meaningful. Before I could greet the man with a "Good morning," Christian interrupted me by grabbing me closely and embracing me with a passionate kiss.

I had to realize what was going on, but, honey, when I did, I fell right in line! I definitely participated by kissing him back, while running my fingers through his hair. Let me tell you something! If this man can't do anything else, his tongue and kissing game is on point. He had just enough spit and tongue action needed to get somebody's blood moving, if you know what I mean. Some people just straight slob in your mouth rather than kiss you!

The kiss lasted awhile, followed by Christian lifting me up on the desk and grinding between my legs. Then all hell broke loose. Man, it turned into rough kissing, strong rubbing on each other, lip smacking, moans, and groans. We were going in!

Suddenly, the doorknob of the classroom door turned! Rushing, I tried to find my shirt and get myself together. I tried to kindly stop Christian, but he was so gone, I had to smack him off me. It was the students coming in.

"Good morning, class!" I said to the students.

Christian rubbed his face where I had smacked him and sat in his seat.

"Today is rehearsal, so I'm hoping that everyone studied their parts."

"Yeah, yeah, yeah!" the students said.

"So, without further ado, let's get started!"

The lights were turned low, and everyone was seated. *The Saturday Nighters* was in action. Of course, I started my introduction first!

"Welcome to *The Saturday Nighters*! My name is Alice Dunbar-Nelson, and I love to teach. Teaching is my passion! I was born on July 19, 1875. I was married three times, but out of all of my marriages, my last marriage was my true love. His name was Paul Laurence Dunbar!"

Christian, as Paul Laurence Dunbar, proceeded to introduce his profile. "I was born on July 27, 1872. My occupations are the following: an American poet, novelist, and playwright of the late nineteenth and early twentieth centuries. As you know, I was married to the beautiful Alice Dunbar-Nelson. I called her the sweetest, smartest little girl I ever saw. She was truly the love of my life," Christian said, looking at me seductively.

I looked at him with awe.

"My name is Jean Toomer," Corey Black said as he smoked on a 1920s cigarette. "I was born on December 26, 1894, and died on March 30, 1967. I was raised in Washington, DC. My occupations are as follows: playwright, author, and poet."

"Langston Hughes is the name, and I'm the star of the show!" Eman Jafar said. "I made the Harlem Renaissance. I was born on February 1, 1902. My occupation is an American poet, social activist, novelist, playwright, and columnist from Joplin, Missouri. I died on May 22, 1967, in New York City at the age of sixty-five from complications after abdominal surgery related to prostate cancer," Eman finished.

"Hi, my name is Esther Popel," Kia Mason introduced herself. "I was born on July 16, 1896, in Harrisburg, Pennsylvania. I am an African American poet, activist, and educator. I pursued the Latin scientific curriculum, which emphasized Latin and modern languages, such as French, German, and Spanish. To conclude, I am a very religious individual."

The last student, Catrina Askew, stood up and introduced herself. "Hello, my name is Effie Lee Lawson, and I am an educator of the African American race and basic knowledge.

"Wonderful, but on the actual day, I would like it if you thoroughly got into character, like, tell us something dark, secretive, and juicy. Tell us something about your character that will make our heads turn and do a double take. Relate to them as much as you can. Let them take you away."

The bell rang for dismissal. I said, "Until next class! Please make sure that you study, study, study, and rehearse your profile please!"

When the classroom was clear, Christian came up behind me and put his arm around my waist tightly. He caressed my neck with his soft, delicate lips.

"I want to take you out," Christian said as he slowly licked my earlobe.

"Well, it depends on if you are trying to take me out in the bedroom!" I said as I turned around. Wrapping my hands around his neck, I looked him straight in the eye.

"For now, out, like tonight and tomorrow, going on a camping trip on the Mississippi River under the stars, warm campfire, smoked marshmallows, and good cuddling," Christian said, cuddling up under me more.

"Mmmm, okay, it's a date," I agreed.

"Well, I'll pick you up tonight at seven, stay until Saturday, then leave Sunday at four," Christian explained.

"Sounds good!" I said, as I kissed him goodbye and left the classroom.

Melting slowly, I walked out the door and left for home. I packed something short and tight for nightwear to pique his interest. I also included campfire attire and some things I might need to survive the natural environment.

At 7:00 p.m. on the dot, Christian pulled up and knocked on the door. I answered and greeted him, and we went on our way. We arrived at the camping site and started unpacking.

Christian started to construct the tent and make the fire.

After forty-five minutes, everything was in tip-top shape and we were ready to start our camping experience.

We were opening up to each other about feelings, romance, beliefs, and assurance.

Christian asked as we were cuddling, "Now that we are alone, how do you really feel about me, Makira?"

My heart dropped to my stomach as I said, "I do have strong feelings for you, Christian. It's just hard for me to express them because of my beliefs."

"Now be sure; are they your beliefs or your father's beliefs?" Christian said.

"I don't know," I said, pressing my face into his chest.

"I will always be here for you, Makira," Christian said, as he continued to hold me.

The next day, we went out on a hiking trial. We discovered animals and did camping activities. At three in the afternoon, we packed up!

Christian started to act strange. I felt him just looking at me as I kept packing.

Then, he came up behind me, turned me around, and told me, "I love you, Makira!"

Y'all, I swear I peed a little in my pants.

CHAPTER 11

The Quiet Storm, Final Hour

I woke up happy, like never before. I felt new and whole. With a smile painted on my face, I grabbed my phone off the nightstand and looked at it.

There was a missed text message from Christian that read, "Good morning, my love!"

I was all in my feelings, y'all!

"Good morning, handsome! Is it possible that you can meet me at the school to prep for the play?" I texted Christian.

"Anything you want, my queen!" Christian sent with a crown emoji.

"That's what I'm talking about! Bow down to the queen!"

I threw on my Nike jogging suit, revealing all my curves. You know, girls, the jogging pants that make your butt look extra big and jiggly!

I left the house looking flawless.

I hopped in the car and drove to the job. I entered the university and went to my office.

Out of nowhere, Christian creeped up behind me and whispered softly in my ear, "Now who are you wearing that for? You know what those pants do to me!" He grabbed a chunk of my thigh and squeezed it as he bit his bottom lip.

"I know; that's why I am wearing them," I responded.

Seductively, I reached back and rubbed the back of his head as he kissed my neck. Desperately, I turned around and started kissing him roughly.

Christian rubbed up my shirt as I started to take his shirt off!

"Oh my God!" Out of nowhere, my father entered the room and was shocked at what he was seeing. He cleared his throat to get our attention.

"Daddy!" I shouted with a high-pitched voice, embarrassed that my father had caught me kissing the enemy. This went against his beliefs.

"What the hell is going on in here?" Daddy said angrily.

"Nothing, Daddy! Something was on my face!" I lied.

"Yeah, Christian!"

"Daddy, you know that that is against everything we believe in. Come on, Daddy! It's me. Your daughter here!" I told him.

"Well, I guess my eyes are deceiving me!" he said to me. "You should know your place, Christian!" he said to Christian.

"And you should know yours!" Christian clapped back.

Upset, Daddy called me out in the hallway!

"Makira, I am ashamed of you! How could you do this to me! Everything I taught you, our beliefs!" he said angrily to me.

"What happened to, quote unquote, it's good to change!" I reminded him.

"Not when it comes down to my daughter and that type of change! I forbid it. I will not have any half breeds as my grandchildren!" he demanded.

"Fine, it will never happen again," I said, as I reentered the classroom with Christian and slammed the door.

"We can't do this anymore!" I explained to Christian.

"*What*! Because of some crap your father just said to you? This is bull!" Christian said, turning red.

"Look, it's not like that, Christian!" I said.

"It's about you and me!" He grabbed my hands and kissed them both.

"Right?" he asked as he lifted my head up.

I didn't reply.

Angry as ever, Daddy went to his office and called T. J., his right-hand man, Sapphire's ex-boyfriend.

"Hello?" T. J. said.

"We've got a problem," Daddy proclaimed. "It seems like my daughter is catching jungle fever, and we can't have that! So, I need you to come in and play matchmaker."

"*What*!" T. J. responded.

"Come on; you owe me one!" Daddy said to T. J.

"I think that we are even. I gave you what you wanted. What else do you want—blood?" T. J. asked.

"I'll think about it! What I want you to do for now is to date my daughter. Treat her good but no sex. I want my daughter to stay pure. I'll pay you good!" he said with a mischievous smile.

"You have really lost your mind! You want me to date your daughter but not have sex with her. You have really lost your mind! Where is the pleasure?" T. J. said.

"Dating my daughter is pleasure and a privilege!" Daddy claimed.

"Look. No offense, but your daughter is not my type. She is hardheaded and has too many opinions and beliefs. She's bossy and judgmental!" T. J. finished.

"I don't care what you think about her. Just do it or else!" Daddy demanded and slammed the phone down.

T. J. shook his head and went back to what he was doing.

Back to me and Christian, I went back into the classroom, and the tension was in the air for real!

I kept looking at Christian, feeling sorry.

Christian was still red and upset after ten minutes of sitting in complete silence. I broke the silence.

"Look, I'm sorry for what happened today," I said, looking at him.

Christian, in his feelings, paid me no mind.

One thing y'all need to know about me is I hate when people I really care about are mad with me! I have to make it right. I couldn't have my baby daddy mad at me, y'all!

"Meet me at the Ohr-O'Keefe Museum of Art tonight at eleven!" I said as I walked out of the classroom seductively. It was that time, y'all!

It was eleven, and Christian had made his way there by following the arrows that were set aside for him.

When he got to the main gallery of the museum, there was a big sign that said, "Presenting the Black Queen!"

Christian walked in, mesmerized by what he saw—me, my beautiful, bare, half-painted, glossy red-and-orange body, with two round cheeks staring at him.

Stunned, Christian stared. I loved it! He was anxious, paralyzed by my full-figured body. I loved the attention! Everything was right!

The light from the moon illuminated my form. I was the best exhibit in that whole museum, ya hear me! I had my favorite artist,

Erykah Badu, playing in the background, "U Got Me." I was in my zone! I started twerking slowly for my baby!

Christian was fascinated!

Like a thief in the night, I came up on him and pulled his jacket off slowly, fighting his tongue with mine as we kissed.

Christian started unbuckling his pants, as he licked my neck.

"I got you, baby!" I finished unbuckling his pants and pulled them down.

"What is this?" I asked.

"What you mean, what is this?

"Fool! Don't try to play me! Where is the rest of it!" I questioned.

"You got a lot to learn! Size doesn't matter! It's all about the motion of the ocean!" Christian proclaimed.

I was thinking, *He can't do nothing with that thang! This whole time, I'm thinking he was packing!* He was half full, y'all!

"Show me!" I walked to the paint buckets.

I grabbed the paintbrush and examined his body before painting. Inspired, I started from his face and moved to his midsection and down to his toes. Forty-five minutes later, I was finished!

Christian was coated in three coats of black matte, glossy, and regular black paint. Black Panther ain't got nothing on my baby! That muscular chest and arms painted in black, y'all! Yaaasss!

He looked at me to see what my next move would be.

I recoated my body with red and orange paint. Then, I walked to the center of the big painting paper that I had laid on the floor.

"Let's make our own art!" I said as I assumed the position.

From that point, Christian shut me up! He worshipped me—defining the word *foreplay*! Then came the time of truth! I'ma tell you right now, he did his thang!

He made me eat those words!

After two hours of back scratching, pain, pressure, pleasure, and sweat-drenched bodies joined to each other, lifeless, we both fell into a deep slumber, holding each other.

Dawn's rays broke on our bodies.

"It's morning, baby," I said.

"What a gorgeous sight to see when you wake up," Christian said and kissed me.

And, the drama queen I am, I didn't even mind the morning breath! That's real love, y'all! I am sprung!

"I want to show you something," I said to Christian.

"Look at my innocence! Look at the natural paint from our bodies! Look at our body painting overall! I will treasure this! It's special to me!" I rolled up the big picture we made.

See, people don't understand that when two bodies become as one, it's really an emotional thing! It takes that right one to activate your body—the reaction and attraction!

"Let's go back to my place and wash up!" I recommended.

"That sounds good, as long as we can do it together!" Christian said.

"It's fine with me!" I confirmed.

We left the gallery and went to my place to wash.

Once we arrived, we jumped into the shower and then laid in bed as we held each other.

Three hours passed, and I heard a knock at my door. I hurried to put on my pink silk robe and went downstairs.

"T. J., wow, what are you doing here?" I said, surprised.

"Just wanted to come by and say hello!" T. J. said.

"Oh, okay, everything is going well, but right now is not a good time for me to talk! Can you come back some other time?" I said, trying to push him away.

"Well, I won't be long!" he said as he let himself in. "I love the robe by the way! You have a special guest here?"

"And if I did, it's none of your business!" I said angrily.

"Relax! You are so uptight," T. J. announced.

"What do you really want, T. J.?" I asked.

"I have a confession to make," T. J. stated. "This is not easy to say, but I was always very fond of you!" He rubbed my arm.

"What the hell are you talking about, T. J.?" I said as I snatched my arm away from him. "You used to be madly in love with Sapphire. Now you are in here telling me that you were always fond of me? Get the hell out!" I shouted.

Suddenly, T. J. grabbed my arm and pulled me close to him.

"Get your hands off me!" I screamed out.

"What the hell are you doing?" Christian said as he pushed him to the wall.

"Have you lost your mind, white boy?" T. J. said as he pushed Christian off him.

"No, but you have!" Christian said and punched T. J. in the face.

Christian and T. J. began to fight, breaking tables, throwing each other into the walls, and so on. The fight went from bad to worse.

T. J. got in a couple of hits, until Christian threw T. J. on the ground, got on top of him, and started bashing T. J.'s face in with his fist.

Christian was covered with T. J.'s blood.

"Stop it, Christian! You're going to kill him," I said as I grabbed Christian's fist.

"You're not even worth it!" Christian said as he got the last hit in and then kicked T. J.

Christian walked back up the stairs.

"I want you to get out *now*, T. J.! Get out of *my house!*" I screamed out.

T. J. was in a daze as he stumbled out of the house.

After I cleaned the mess up, I went upstairs to check on Christian.

I saw him on the edge of the bed, sitting there with his whole body red.

I climbed behind him and started rubbing on his shoulder.

"What was that all about?" Christian asked.

"I don't even know what that was all about," I answered.

"He said that he has always had a little thang for you! So are you trying to play me, Makira?" Christian said.

71

"No, Christian! I don't have any feelings whatsoever for T. J. He used to date my best friend, Sapphire. I don't know what type of power trip crap he is on right now!" I said.

"Maybe he really wanted you instead of Sapphire," Christian stated.

"Christian, stop it now. I don't care about T. J. like that. I care about you! You are the one I gave my virginity to. It's you that I want!" I rubbed his face. "Please, let's put this behind us! Speaking of behind, did you enjoy yourself?" I asked as I licked his ear.

"Hell, yeah!" He kissed my neck.

"Why don't you go home, get a change of clothes, and meet me at this address!" I whispered in his ear. "I'll make it worth your while!" I explained

"Okay!" Christian said as he walked downstairs and let himself out.

The Monument Historic Inn, Natchez, Mississippi, was the address I gave Christian.

When I got to the hotel, I decorated the room like a jail cell. Minutes later, Christian knocked on the door.

My sexy self went to the door with a two-piece lingerie thong set on and a cop hat! I hid behind the door as Christian entered looking for me. I shut the door and seductively smiled at him.

He walked up to me and held me. Before he could kiss me, I put my finger on his lips.

Christian moved my finger and said, "I can't wait to see what creative, spontaneous thing you have planned tonight."

"Well, sit back and relax! Oh, but before you do, put on this black mask with these black sweat pants, and this long-sleeve black shirt!"

"Wait. What? I can see the mask, but the rest of this stuff is not sexy?" Christian said, confused.

"Well, we will be role playing, cops and robbers!" I said, pulling him into the bed.

"Look, I'm not feeling this costume! Why don't we just be ourselves tonight?" Christian suggested.

"Okay, well, I will assume the position!" I said

"No, I want to see your beautiful face!" Christian exclaimed.

"Or I can turn around and let you see this booty move!" I suggested.

"Okay, cut the crap, Makira, no paint, no mask, no type of covering. I'ma just come as myself!" Christian explained as he got in the bed. "Come on, Makira; you love me, right? For me?"

I stood stiff, trying to move to the bed where Christian was, but I looked up at him with sorrow. The tears started to show my true motive.

I just couldn't see physically with my eyes a white man making love to me, even though it was extremely good and I had real, genuine feelings for him! Okay, I loved him! You happy now! I couldn't do it, y'all! My daddy would hate me, and my daddy was all I had!

I couldn't see with my eyes that I was making love to this pale man, the enemy, this white man! It went against my beliefs."

"You can do it, can you?" Christian asked me.

"I'm a fool! You got me thinking you're being romantic and creative, but in reality, you're covering my skin so you can be more comfortable with making love to me. "I forgot, I have to be black!"

"I guess that's why you always want to be on all fours! To show me how much of a dog you really are?" Christian said as he left, slamming the door behind him!

CHAPTER 12

Redemption

It was eight thirty in the evening, and Sapphire was just coming from a Black Panther meeting. She drove to her home.

She entered the house, and her real husband greeted her. "How was the meeting?" he said as he was reading a book.

"Well, as always, inspirational and moving. The topic was about how to get gun violence in black-on-black crime eliminated," Sapphire said as she put her purse on the counter.

"That dress is a little short, don't you think?" her husband said. "That's not what I picked out for you this morning," he said angrily.

"Yeah, what you picked out earlier looked a hot mess," Sapphire said, walking away *until* he grabbed her and said, "You are my woman. I own you! You are pregnant with my baby," holding her tightly.

"You are not my daddy! You don't own me! You need to know your place!" She snatched her arm away from him. "Get off me!" Sapphire walked away.

He turned her around and smacked her down to the ground. Sapphire shouted out in pain as she fell to the ground.

"You need to know your place! He said

Poor Sapphire just sat on the floor stunned. He picked Sapphire up, took her to the bedroom, and laid her in the bed.

Sapphire woke up the next morning to a black left eye. To cover the abuse, she packed on concealer and Mac lipstick. Dressed in a long maxi dress, she proceeded out the door to Oliver Johnson University.

When she got to the university, she finished cleaning some paperwork out of her desk. She intended to go to *The Saturday Nighters* play.

Knock, knock, knock.

Sapphire answered the door and said, "T. J., what are you doing here?"

"Today is the big day, *The Saturday Nighters* play!" T. J. explained.

"I know. That's why I'm here and also to pick up some things out the office."

T. J. looked her up and down and said, "You look good."

"Yeah, I'm pregnant, can't see my feet, and have a black left eye," she said as she snatched her sunglasses off to show T. J. "Yeah, I do look real good! Get out of here! It's all your fault! You are a sorry excuse for a man! *Get out!*" Sapphire screamed at T. J. as she held on to the desk crying.

T. J. left the office, heartbroken and outraged at what had happened to Sapphire. He went into the classroom and just sat there in a rage.

Christian's father, Jonathan, entered the classroom and saw T. J. He said, "So things are not greener on the other side, are they?"

T. J. looked up angrily and said, "You don't know what you are talking about."

"I know exactly what I'm talking about! I can help you from here. You don't need him anymore. Expose him for who he really is," Jonathan said as he looked T. J. straight in the eye.

Later that day, the students started to arrive, dressed up and ready to perform.

Christian and I met up in the hallway. He tried so hard not to acknowledge me it was pathetic.

I sped up to catch up with him and said, "Christian, wait! I just wanted to—"

Before I could finish my sentence, Christian cut me off and said, "Save it! I have heard it all before. For now, let's just keep it professional. You can handle that better!" he said before storming away from me into the classroom.

Hurt and humiliated, I went into the classroom silently with a heavy heart. The classroom was dark and looked identical to a 1920s club in Harlem. Smoke from long cigarettes filled the room. Live jazz music played in the background.

"Welcome, audience, my name is Alice Dunbar-Nelson, and I will be your host for tonight," I said. "Once again, welcome to *The Saturday Nighters*, where beliefs are expressed and the truth is revealed. We are more than black African Americans! We are strong, knowledgeable, creative, and enthusiastic individuals who strive for only the best and nothing less.

"I am Alice Dunbar-Nelson, formerly married to Paul Laurence Dunbar! What a man! What a man!" I looked straight at Christian. "Born on July 19, 1875, I was an activist for civil rights as a poet, journalist, short-story writer, and playwright. My works include *Violets and Other Tales* and *The Goodness of St. Rocque and Other Stories.* I am also known for portraying the complicated reality of an African American woman and intellectuals, addressing topics such as racism, oppression, family, work, and sexuality.

"I have this deep, dark secret! I have been accused of having a long same-sex relationship with Principal Edwina Brouse at Howard High School in Wilmington.

"I married my third husband, Robert Nelson, in 1916. My husband learned of my extramarital lesbian relations—including those with journalist Fay Jackson Robinson and artist Helen London by reading my diary. I apologized to him for tolerating these alleged affairs. Despite the affairs, my marriage lasted until my death. I died of heart failure in 1935. One of my poems that I treasured the most is called 'If I had Known.' This poem is basically about a woman who wished that she knew what life would be like before she actually had to go through it. Now, I do have a heterosexual issue with a guy who is white. It shouldn't be this way because I love him, but I'm just trying to protect my image!" I said as I looked directly at Christian with tears of sorrow in my eyes.

Everyone clapped.

"Good evening, my name is Paul Laurence. I was born on June 27, 1872. I am an American poet, novelist, and playwright of the late nineteenth and early twentieth centuries. I am a graduate of Straight University, a historically black college.

"My sweet secret is Alice Dunbar. I call her the sweetest, smartest little girl I ever saw! We wrote books of poetry as comparison pieces. A token of our love, 'Life and Marriage,' was portrayed in *Oak and Ivory*, a 2001 play by Kathleen McGree Anderson.

Looking at me, Christian said, "The love we share is secret and unique!"

He took my hand and then out of nowhere laid a big kiss on my lips. I swear this dude has a little black in him! "He is just straight hood! Everyone was shocked, gasping for air. We finished our long-awaited kiss in front of everyone, including my father, Oliver Johnson.

He was outraged in his seat.

"This is one of my favorite poems. It relates to a lot of individuals around me—i.e., haters!" Christian looked around, especially at my daddy! "'We Wear the Mask'—this poem is about people, like some of you in here, wearing a veil over your face to be impressive or impress other people. It means that you don't have a mind of your own! Christian said, and he sat down.

"Wow, that was good and true!" Eman Jafar said. "Well, everyone should know me as the one and only Langston Hughes! I was born on February 1, 1902. You know what that means, Aquarius season! I'm very creative, spontaneous, and imaginative.

"I absolutely love going out the box and doing things most people wouldn't do. I am an American poet, social activist, novelist, playwright, and columnist from Joplin, Missouri. I was one of the earliest innovators of the new literary art form called jazz poetry. I am best known as a leader of the Harlem Renaissance in New York City. Speaking of 'We Wear the Mask,' I am a *homosexual*. I, Eman Jafar, have done some things that I'm definitely not proud of, but my flesh loved it.

"I remember I was a little boy, and my father, a pastor, always had his other pastor friends over on Sundays after church.

"At the age of twelve, I was shaped different from other boys. God blessed this light-skinned bowl of fineness with a beautiful, hand-chiseled, structured faced and round bottom that no one could refuse. I had a bigger bottom than your average twenty-six-year-old woman!

"Anyway, my father's pastor friends would come over and sit, laugh, and talk about their sermons at their church. It was my father's best friend, Steven Moral. He used to watch the way I walked and talked up until the day he stopped watching and took action.

I felt Eman Jafar's pain and saw the tears forming in his eyes! He had put his head down, and tears began to fall down as he continued to explain his story!

"For the first time in my life, I had received oral sex—in the bathroom from this man. I was confused and felt dirty! After the fact, I tried to tell my father, but he didn't listen. He smacked me and said, 'Get out of my face, you faggot!'

"I wanted to tell my mother, but she was one of those submissive wives—the my-husband-is-always-right type of wife—so I didn't even try to tell her. My father's best friend, Steven Moral, started to buy me expensive things and eventually wanted more for his money! Brainwashed at this point with unsupportive parents, I gave him what he wanted! It first started with him, and then I got gang banged by *all* of Steven Moral friends

"To this day, I am very confused about my sexuality! I tried having sex with a woman and got disgusted. I pray to God to help me and to send me a real pastor, a man of God, to guide me. Moving on!" Eman said as he wiped his face. He went on with his profile.

"One of my favorite poems is called 'Evil'! The poem describes someone you want so bad, who is playing hard to get!" When Eman Jafar sat down, he got a standing ovation.

Corey Black stood up and said, "It's getting real in here! My name is Jean Toomer, and I believe that hard, manual work and dedication make you a man! See, see, see, we didn't have all these new, high-tech gadgets in my day. *No!* We had only these!" Corey Black had put up two fists in the air.

"These were money makers, our prize possession! We worked through the week and earned a reasonable wage at the end of the week! What's wrong with this new generation is that they want so much but do so little! I was born on December 26, 1894, in Washington, DC. My occupations are as follows: playwright, author, and poet. I was raised by my mother and grandmother, because my father left us.

"As stated, my name is Corey Black, and I am a fatherless child. My father left my mother while she was giving birth to me. He said he found someone new and, quote unquote, *improved*. That woman was also pregnant with his child and gave birth to him the same time my mother gave birth to me.

"My mother coming out of the hospital had no money and no job because my father was the breadwinner of the family, so we moved from a two-story home into a roach-infested motel called public housing! So, while we were being bitten by the roaches, him and his son was living the good life.

"I went to school with his son, and his son used to pick on me and always brag about his chains and necklaces because he was a petty drug dealer selling dope in the other neighborhoods. I got tired of the food stamps and him bragging, and I started to sell dope in my neighborhood. I was bad, y'all!

"I started to top his profits and bring in new revenue! I was the man in the streets! I had different females throwing themselves at me left and right—including that freak that man had left me and my mom for! She would always say how handsome I was and trying to sleep with me. She was a crackhead and a ho! I got head from her just to make that sperm donor and his son mad!

"I remember it like it was yesterday, when he came in my turf, mad as ever, acting like a real live gangsta, when he really was just a runner! I beat the brakes off him and took his chain! Furious and embarrassed, he went up to New York and started slanging dope. Trouble in paradise with that freak and my sperm donor! He caught her having sex in his house with the local drug dealers, police officers, you name it! Every time he would kick her out, she would find herself back in his heart! Then the most trifling thing happened! The sperm donor caught his son and his freak having sex! It was crazy yo! To make a long story short, that same night they got caught, my sperm donor died by the hands of his own son, and the freak and his son cleared his bank account and took everything the sperm donor owned and left for New York! They eventually got caught and got life in prison!

"Anyway, back to me, I was in and out of jail, putting my mother through more hell! She stayed by my side the whole way though! Not missing a beat! What really changed me is when I had my first child at the age of eighteen years old! It was a boy! I didn't want to be like that sperm donor! Not being a part of my child's life! I love my mother, and my baby mother, and I wanted to do right by them.

"Getting out of jail, me and baby mother married and went through our financial ups and downs! I worked three jobs to make ends meet to support my family, living in an apartment that was going to fall down any minute and a turn-up, raggedy car.

"Yeah, I was about that life, but look at me now! I'm twenty-six, have a relationship with God, have my own company, good credit, a house built from the ground up, and the car of my dreams!

"Why am I saying this? Because when life throws you a curve ball, how are you going to hit? Will you be focused and hit a home run or just stand there and let it pass you by and be full of frustration and anger? Being a black man is hard, and there is always a naysayer in the background. Dreams, a relationship with God, hard work, dedication, being self-driven, and having leaders by your side is nothing but success! One of my favorite poems is called 'Reapers' by Jean Toomer. To break this poem down when analyzing, the general objective or sum of this poem is to make a difference in our society by helping one another. It is a developing process, but, one by one, it will be a project of success. Going back to the poem, in the first scene, it says, 'Work is done by humans and hand tools,' meaning, it takes more than one reaper to do the job; doing work by hand requires more workers and therefore builds or sustains a community.

"Now in scene two, it is totally the opposite. In the second scene, it says, 'Only a mindless machine pulled by mindless animals,' which is behaviors, explaining a heartless individual with no sense of purpose and no human sensibilities.

"A machine cannot react to a squeal of pain or a stain of blood, but it does know what to destroy, and it would not care at all! Perfect example, the massive killing in Las Vegas, the white-on-black crime, the black-on-black crime, the killings in the churches, and the killings in the schools are mindless machine killings! There's no conscious thought, no better judgment! It is a deadly virus being rebirthed by the wicked over and over again! Is this the last chapter for society? I shake my head and only pray for God's mercy on this nation! Love covers a multitude of sins!"

As Corey Black took his seat, everyone stood with tears in their eyes.

"Good evening, my name is Effie Lee Newsome," Catrina Askew said. "I was born on January 19, 1955, in Philadelphia, Pennsylvania.

My father, Benjamin Franklin Lee, was an editor of Philadelphia's *Christian Recorder* and a bishop of the African Methodist Episcopal church. I was one of the first African Americans who primarily wrote poems for children. One good example is *Gladiola Garden*, poems of the outdoors and indoors for second-grade readers.

"My poems were to help young readers celebrate their own beauty and recognize themselves in fairy tales, folktales, and nature! One of my favorite poems is 'The Bronze Legacy.' Clearly, we can analyze what it means, but, to specify, it's talking about how young African Americans should be proud of their color and not ashamed. It says, 'The strongest things in the world are brown so they should thank God that they are brown.'"

As Catrina Askew took her seat, Kia stood up and introduced herself. "My name is Esther Popel, and I was born on July 16, 1896, to Joseph Gibbs and Helen King in Harrisburg. I graduated from Central High School in Harrisburg in 1915 and enrolled at Dickson the following fall. I was the first African American woman to enroll in college. I studied French, German, Latin, and Spanish. I received the 1919 John Patton Memorial Prize.

"After graduating in 1919, I married William Andrew Shaw on April 11, 1925, and gave birth to a daughter, Esther Patricia, born June 1, 1926. I started my long career as a teacher but was not only recognized as a teacher but as a poet of the Harlem Renaissance." Kia continued in her own voice, "My most favorite poem of all time is called 'October Prayer' by Esther Popel. It takes me back to my childhood, when my father used to say harsh things to me, verbally, like for instance, 'With yo black self!' He was always making a difference between me and my sister because she was more of a butter pecan and I am more dark chocolate. My father *loved* light-skinned people. He worshipped the ground they walked on! Anyways, the verbal abuse came from my father, the little boys in the neighborhood, and on up in school.

"One thing I used to do to help me cope with living as a dark-skin girl was to play with Barbie dolls. I isolated myself because of my skin deficiency and didn't have many people I could talk to, so I talked to my dolls and made story lines for them. I felt comfortable with them and felt my dolls couldn't hurt me!

"Secondly, I used to make these notebooks called *My Family Book* that had celebrities, video vixens, or beautiful people in my school in them. They represented my imaginary family. I made these family books to recognize everyone was beautiful and can't no one be judged by anyone.

"I pictured myself as Aaliyah Haughton and went by the name of Kitten! My husband was first Jim Jones from Rockafella and then Lloyd from Murder Inc. and so on—until, in middle school, I started to get more attention because of my body appearance and with the crowd I started hanging out with.

"I remember it like it was yesterday; my first crush was in middle school. He was light skinned, had cornrows and beautiful white teeth, and was tall. Out of all the beautiful, drop-dead gorgeous girls, why did he choose me? I was just a butter face, which, back in the day, meant a girl with a nice body and an ugly face! I was not worthy of him!

"He used to say sexual things to me and just say how beautiful I was! It made me feel so good I had to write in a diary everything he would say, or any other boy would say, to build my confidence up! I read it to myself over and over again when I felt low!

"I really started to smell myself, to where I was letting little boys dry hump me behind trees and then letting them finger me and saying stupid somethings in my ear! My hormones were going crazy! I was twice as hot as a dog in heat!

"If I couldn't get a little boy to touch me or say something nice to me, I would watch porn when everyone left the house. My favorite one was the Hentai porn because it was very out the box, it had demons, monsters, and a lot of submission with whips and chains in it. Or if I couldn't get to the porn, I would simulate in my mind my own porn of me being gangbanged by thirty men, me being outside with my legs wide open and strangers just coming in the backyard having sex with me, even stray animals! Long as it walked, I was fine with it! One to two hours, naked, either humping under the bed, on the bathroom floor, on the edge of the sofa arm, on top of the sofa, on top of the kitchen table! Breaking out in severe sweats and just dropping into a deep sleep!

"I remember one day when everyone was out of the house and I was home alone, I used over half of a container of butter on my body, mainly my butt, then stuck my butt out the window. I can laugh now, but I clearly also remember my mom complaining, in her exact words, saying, 'Aye, y'all need to take it easy on the butter; this is the second container this week! What are y'all doing with the butter?' I smiled and left out the kitchen!

"Then I imagined myself as a roasted pig. I got on the table and got in a position of a pig and put an apple in my mouth and just laid there on the table! I got so much sexual pleasure out of it!

"That wasn't enough, so I took it to the next level! The boys and men made me feel so good about myself, I started to make them feel good! I had sex just because they acknowledged how pretty I was, until one day, I was in summer school and went to the bathroom, and in my underwear, there was cottage-cheese-looking discharge in my panties. Yes, it was an STD! It was chlamydia! It definitely slowed me down from having sex until I hit rock bottom again!

"Everyone around me was falling in love, except me! So, I went back out there again, messing with these various men again, all for the wrong reason! Destroying my secret temple! Until one day I ran into my children's father, and it felt like it was perfect. He was everything I dreamed of!

"Years went past, and marriage was not the answer!'

"More years, in the future, we called it quits. From that breakup, I entered numerous beds and heartache and pain from dating sites or just meeting someone on the streets.

"It got so outrageous that I caught HPV! That's when life really hit me! It was like the doctor had told me that I had caught HIV!

"Many nights, I couldn't sleep, researching things about low-risk HPV and high-risk HPV! How there is no cure for the virus, that your immune system has to fight the virus off itself. That HPV causes *cancer*!

"The YouTube commercials online and on TV about how people with HPV were now dealing with cervical cancer and they couldn't get rid of it! Just to see the words on the billboards while I was driving down the streets or on the pharmacy board about getting the shot to prevent HPV made me cry!

"Why, Lord? I know I messed up, but why'd you choose me to have to go through this?

"Day in and day out, I was pulling down my underwear every thirty minutes, looking for bumps on my private parts, heavy discharge, or anything out of the ordinary! I was living in true fear!

"Scared to death, I was taking twelve vitamins a day to help my immune system, exercising, eating right, trying to get my mind off the symptoms of heavy discharge, the irresistible burning sensation, and the itching! I wanted to kill myself. I couldn't live on this earth with this virus! I started to plan the perfect suicide! Then my doctor prayed for me and told me that she was not worried about it and that I shouldn't be either. I would get through this. She also prayed that God would send my Boaz.

"For a year and some months, I dealt with this horrible virus! There was nonstop severe burning, heavy discharge, and itching. No cure, but just having faith in the almighty God!

"I started going back to church and got my life right with God! I realized God was my cure, and for that, he gets all the honor and all the praise, because no man-made medicine on this earth could help me! He is my friend, my husband, my daddy, my everything! Friends couldn't help me at my lowest point! All those men I had sexual intercourse with was gone, and I'm sitting up here in pain! Now look at me! The HPV is gone 100 percent, and I'm married to the love of my life.

"I wrote this poem for my husband!

I Stepped on True Love
I never thought that I would taste the sweet, tangy
taste of true love.
The way his kisses give me butterflies.
The touch of a strong, sexy man overflows me!
To join as one and deliver such great pleasure—
How wonderful is it to finally step on true love!

"God has been opening doors for me! I want to live out of God's hand and worship him, because if it wasn't for him, I would have been dead a long time ago! I could've had HIV!

"I'm happier than I've ever been before. Word of advice to any men or women who are struggling with HPV, please don't give up! Stay strong in the fight, and when God is on your side, you will win no matter how it looks! Build up your immune system by eating right, taking one or two vitamins, and exercising! Having faith and determination brings you a long way! With the men and women who are seeking attention and love, tell yourself you are beautiful despite what others say.

"This is for that little dark-skin girl who is insecure and uncomfortable in her skin. Remind yourself that you are one of a kind! They just want to look like you! I don't care if you are dark skin, light skin, in between, can't nobody love you like you and God can! Don't run after love; let love run after you! Look in the mirror and define for yourself who you are and what you are here for! You have to love yourself before anyone else loves you," Kia said, and she took her seat.

Sapphire stood up, still pregnant, wearing big round sunglasses.

"Good evening to you all! My name is Maya Angelou. I joined the Harlem Writers Guild in the late 1950s. I'm an American poet, storyteller, activist, and autobiographer. I'm also known as a singer, dancer, actress, and composer and the first female black director. I'm most famous as a writer, editor, essayist, playwright, and poet. I've worked for Dr. Martin Luther King Jr. and Malcolm X," Sapphire said. "I was strolling on YouTube and found an interview with Maya Angelou, and it really spoke to me! This is what she said in her interview!

"'In one of my evocative and controversial moments, I described how I was cuddled then raped by my mother's boyfriend when I was seven years old. I recently did an interview about my rape, and this is what I had to say: The rapist was let out of jail and was found dead that night. I thought I had caused the death because I had spoken his name. That was my seven-year-old logic. So I stopped talking for five years. Now, to show you again how out of evil there can come good, in those five years, I read every book in the black library and white library. I memorized Shakespeare, whole plays, fifty sonnets. Never having heard it, I memorized it.

"'When I decided to speak, I had a lot to say and many ways in which to say what I had to say. So out of evil, which was a dive kind of evil, because rape on the body of a young person, more often than not, introduces cynicism, and there is nothing quite so tragic as a young cynic. It means the person has gone from knowing nothing to believing nothing. In my case, I was saved in the muteness and was able to draw from human thoughts, human disappointments and triumphs enough to triumph myself.'"

Tears started to fall from Sapphire's eyes. She kept speaking as she slowly took off her glasses.

All the students gasped and held their mouths in shock.

"I, Sapphire, have been keeping quiet for so long, awaiting the right time to let my best friend and you, my students, know the truth! The man that I loved, grew up with, shared many secrets, shared each other's body, shared interest and beliefs with, together, one of a kind, wanted this fame and glory!" Sapphire said, looking at T. J. "His name is T. J. The man I adore gave me to Oliver Johnson! Oliver Johnson helped him be a better lawyer in return for me! Oliver gave him clients, paid a couple of dues for him, and let his name shine!

"Today, Oliver, I am exposing you for who you are!" Sapphire screamed out. "You want to know who the mystery man is, Makira? It is your father, Oliver Johnson! This baby I'm carrying is Oliver Johnson's baby! I'm am married to this hypocritical, selfish, woman-beater ass! He beats me up if his coffee is too hot, or if I don't wear what he takes out for me, he beats me! I've tried running away, but he always finds me! I'm losing my mind!

"I've been desperate and purposely falling down the stairs to kill me and this baby, hitting my stomach with a steel baseball bat so I can kill this child and myself to get away from this man! Nothing is working!" Sapphire exclaimed. "Mr. Oliver Johnson is not the man you think you know. He is a liar. He says that he doesn't believe in interracial relations, but he is paying to have sex with numerous *white* hookers! I know because I followed him and caught ten STDs! He is doing unhuman sexual activities with them. He is a poser and should not be trusted!"

Oh my god, y'all, this whole time, it was my father! Do you how this made me feel on every level? I'd looked up to this hypocritical man all my life! It was too much to handle!

Everybody in the room was shocked—the negativity, the stares, and the disappointments on everyone's face.

Christian shouted out to Daddy, "It doesn't feel good, does it?"

T. J., in a rage, breathing hard, looked like he could kill Daddy.

Daddy looked around and saw the angry faces. His lies and the demons in the black shadows started to talk to him. His reputation was destroyed. The demons whispered to him, "Do it! Kill yourself! Do it! You've lost all your respect! There's no way out!"

Lifeless and disturbed, he dug in his pocket, and showing no facial expressions, no care, he pulled out his gun and shot himself in the head.

Everyone screamed and ran out of the room.

Sapphire looked at him in disgust and threw the wedding ring onto his lifeless body. With my father's blood splattered all over my face, I just stood there in shock! I didn't hear anything anymore.

Everything was moving in slow motion! Death bells were ringing in my ear as I collapsed on the ground!

Christian picked me up and took me out of the classroom, and I was asleep for two days.

Finally, I got the strength to bury my father! I was in a trance, still isolated from the world. Christian tried to come over and comfort me, but I was just out, far in space. He kissed my forehead and walked away. I cut off my phone and all other ties to the world.

Four days later …

I woke up out of my slumber of depression and entered a new day—no makeup, no mask, only possessing a smile and a wonderful beginning!

I put a silk white robe on to show new pureness and texted Christian.

"Meet me at the Mississippi flower field, the one with all the freshly blossomed white flowers."

I left and proceeded to the flower field. The smell of the sweet breeze made me release myself from my robe, and I ran through the flower field bare and uncovered from anything that could hold me back. For the first time in my life, I was free.

Christian saw me from afar. He smiled, took off his clothes as well, and started running in the flower field with me. I looked back at him and ran even faster! He eventually caught up with me, and we fell to the ground in laughter.

I turned around and faced him. I rubbed his face and said, "I love you, and I'm sorry that I put you through all this. I want you to make love to me with no mask." I smiled at Christian, and he smiled back at me.

Christian passionately kissed me, and we made passionate love to each other.

Two weeks later …

After a few days of sharing time with my love, my boo, I had to return to the school to clear the air. As soon as I got to the school, the flashback hit me! I took my hand back from the doorknob.

Christian grabbed me and hugged me. After I got myself together, we went into the classroom.

A bad aroma of death surrounded me. My last time in the classroom, I walked to the podium to release my last words online and to my students. Everyone was gloomy, and the air held the stench of death and sorrow.

I started to cry as I began to speak. "I would say good afternoon, but this room says otherwise! Words can't describe how I feel right now. My God, this has truly been a phenomenal lesson lecture. I asked each and every one of you what emancipation from slavery means to you but never asked myself. My late father"—I paused and started to cry again—"Oliver Johnson manufactured artificial beliefs, suggestions, and characteristics in me, but no more will I believe stupidity. For God gave us are own mind to make our own decision. My father, around others, hated white people but behind closed doors had a tolerance for them for his own selfish needs. I am now free from thinking like him. I am free from slavery."

"We all are!" The class stood up in an uproar of happiness.

After my speech, I went to my office and found an envelope on my desk. It was from Sapphire! So happy and relieved, I sat down and read the letter.

> Good afternoon, Makira. I have to say that your story was encouraging and that you have evolved! You have finally realized your purpose and stopped looking through your father's eyes and looked through your own! What a beautiful day it is! I have given birth to your baby sister and am saddened to say that she was born with abnormalities because

of the rage I withheld in myself for so long and my careless actions. I have sent her to a group home for disabled children. I can't bear to see what my actions and bad memories have cost!

I am Sister Sapphire now and have changed my negative to positive! I'm giving back to my community and spreading the Good News about the Lord. I am now encouraging younger and older adult women who are being sexually abused, controlled, manipulated, and much more to stand up for themselves. I used my last dime to start a youth and adult shelter for runaway women. It's going great!

Well, my love, I'm not going to hold you long, but I just want to say keep up the good work to you and Kia! You have finally realized that love is without color!

Printed in the United States
By Bookmasters